PROTECTING HIS QUEEN

KINGS OF SYDNEY

BOOK ONE

KHLOE WREN

ISBN ebook: 978-1-992942-13-1
ISBN print: 978-1-992942-12-8

Cover Credits:
Digital Artist: Khloe Wren
Model: Jose Barreiro
Photographer: JW Photography & Covers

Editing Credits:
Editor: Carolyn Depew of Write Right Edits
Proofreader: Flourish Books

AUTHOR NOTE

This story takes place in Sydney, New South Wales, Australia, so I've written it in my native language: Australian English. This is similar to British English but with some bonuses! It's a little different to US English, so please keep this in mind while reading.

CHAPTER ONE

Daniil strolled through the Bondi Markets with his relaxed façade firmly in place despite the fact he was anything but. Even though it was Sunday, and he was dressed as casually as he got, in his favourite pair of black jeans, grey cowboy boots and a button up black shirt, he was working, just like all these stall holders around him. Glancing at the cheap, mass-produced jewellery on a table he was passing, he wondered how the hell some of these people made any money at all. So many stores selling the same shit, and there were only so many tourists to go around. With a mental shrug, he kept moving, his gaze roaming as he searched for his target.

While most people didn't recognise him

or know who he was, everyone was quick to get out of his way. Casual for him was still a lot fancier than most people here. His slicked-back steel grey hair and ice-blue eyes, together with his scowl, helped get the message across that he was not someone to be messed with. Daniil had never been a patient man, and he was more than happy to not have to push through the crowd as he moved around the lanes of Bondi's weekly markets.

It was only September, but with no clouds in the sky, the spring sun was powerful, and it wasn't long before he was rolling up his sleeves to cool off. He was grateful he hadn't donned a tie. He rarely did. He hated how they made him feel as though he was being strangled.

Once he revealed his forearms and their tattoos, people were even faster to move out of his way. Thanks to the internet, along with various movies and TV shows, a lot more of the general population was aware of what Russian tattoos looked like, which was both a blessing and a curse. But on days like today, it was a good thing, especially now the day was heating up. Daniil wanted to get this job done so he could get out of the sun.

Unlike many of his brethren, he'd not inked his hands, so when he did need to go under the radar, he simply made sure his arms were fully covered. If he also added dark glasses like he had today, to hide his blue eyes, no one would guess he was even Russian, let alone part of Sydney's underbelly. Some jobs were considerably simpler if no one paid him much attention. It meant he wouldn't have to pay off or blackmail anyone who remembered him accurately enough to be able to tell the cops about him. Since he was only doing some recon today, he didn't need to keep his ink covered.

Reaching the end of the lane, he turned to head down the next one when he caught sight of his target. Stupid bastard was strolling around without a care in the world, as though he owned the joint. No way did that piece of shit realise what was about to happen to him. That thought had Daniil smirking. He loved what he did, especially jobs like this one. Taking out a man who was so convinced he'd made himself invincible enough to get away with whatever bullshit he wanted to pull.

Over the years, Daniil had discovered very few men were truly invincible. Most had a weakness, like this arsehole Daniil was currently trailing. The man's wife and son were with him, the woman stopping to look at trinkets as they moved along. While she was distracted, he was checking out the legs on the young woman running the store. Daniil rolled his eyes. He never could believe how many men would settle down and get married, only to screw around on their wives.

While Daniil had zero interest in getting married or having a family, if he ever changed his mind, he would be one hundred percent committed and faithful. But settling down would give him way too much to lose. It would also prevent him from being able to simply fuck whoever caught his eye, and then move on. He'd never once cuddled or slept with his lovers after sex. He certainly had never brought them to his home, and he never, ever fucked the same woman more than once.

In the weeks Daniil had been studying

this particular target, he'd learned the arsehole had several mistresses. Hell, Daniil was doing the wife a favour by taking him out. Maybe he should contact her, see if she'd pay him as well as the original client for ending him? Shaking his head, he moved away from them. The last thing he needed was his target to spot him before he was ready to show himself. He had a plan forming in his mind on how this one would play out, but it wasn't solid enough to act on yet, because, like most of his jobs, he wasn't being paid to simply kill. The true goal of most of his assignments was to gain something. Money, information ... always something. This was no different. And the way the target kept his palm wrapped around his young son's shoulder made it perfectly clear what, or rather who, Daniil needed to use to get what the client required from this particular target.

Daniil had worked long and hard to gain his reputation, both in his legitimate business dealings and his illegal ones. When it came to his dirtier work, like this current job, he was known as the soulless one. He would, and did, just about anything for money. However, the reality was there were a few lines he refused to cross. One of those was hurting an innocent. So, even though he intended to use the boy against his father, he wouldn't harm one hair on the lad's head. Nope, he was confident he could make the target believe he intended to hurt the child without actually doing so. Because even though he'd never injure an innocent child or woman, he'd cultivated enough rumours about himself that others didn't know he operated by that rule. Hopefully, the threat of harm to the target's son would be enough. If not, he would indeed kidnap the boy, but he wouldn't be hurt.

A stall caught Daniil's eye, and he stopped to take a better look. The photography was stunning, both black-and-whites and coloured images from around Bondi and Sydney, all neatly showcased in professional looking black frames. One in particular caught his attention. It was of an old warehouse a few suburbs away. He nodded as his plan solidified in his mind. He would pay off one of the target's mistresses to not be in their usual hotel room, then he would wait for him in her place. Deliver the threat on his son and get the information his client required before leaving the man to think he'd escaped death. Then, the next morning, Daniil would return to grab him as he left for work before taking him to that abandoned warehouse to finish the job. It wouldn't be the first time he'd used it for this purpose, and he doubted it would be the last.

"Morning. I love that shot. Totally found that place by accident when I caught the wrong bus a few weeks ago."

A shiver ran down his spine at the sound of her sweet voice. It had been a long time since he'd felt anything more than passing lust for a beautiful woman, and he'd certainly never reacted to the mere sound of her uttering a few words. His strange reaction had him curious about the female who'd spoken. Forcing a smile, he turned to face her. Once he caught sight of her, his grin turned genuine. She was stunning. Her hair was a shockingly bright mix of blue and purple that looked good on her. She was shorter than his six feet; he guessed her to be about five feet six inches.

Because God was good, he got an excellent view of her toned and lean body, as all she wore was a bikini top under an open over-shirt. She'd pushed up the sleeves and her skin was tanned and ink free. The bright blue of her bikini matched her hair and drew his eyes to her breasts, which looked lush and natural. He was shocked when his fingers actually twitched with his desire to touch her.

Clearing his throat, he reached up to take his sunglasses off, grateful the dark lenses had prevented her from catching him checking her out just now.

♛

Juli nearly swallowed her tongue. Holy smokes, this dude was hot. Scary as fuck and a lot older than her, but still hot as hell.

"And what was a beauty such as yourself doing alone on a bus?"

Yeah, because his good looks weren't enough, the bastard had a to-die-for accent, too. Life just wasn't fair some days. Her fiancé was so average, it hurt. He didn't have a romantic bone in his body, no cool accent, no ink. Just oil-stained hands from working on cars and cute dimples that had sucked her right in when she'd first met him.

"I often catch the bus. It's cheap and does the job."

He frowned at her like she was nuts. Not an uncommon reaction. Lots of people thought she was crazy, including her fiancé.

"Job?"

"You know? Gets me from A to B?" She grinned at him. "Sometimes it even gets me back to A again."

He shook his head with a chuckle. The sound shot down her spine and made her nipples tighten. Damn, she hoped he didn't notice. It wasn't like her bikini had padding or anything to hide the fact. With a raised eyebrow, his gaze lowered for a moment. Bugger. Of course, he'd noticed. Ah, well, not much she could do about it. Not her fault the man could melt a girl's knickers at twenty paces.

"So, where's your accent from? Europe somewhere?"

"It's Russian."

She nodded like she knew all about various accents and where they came from, even though she had no clue. "Should have guessed that. You visiting, or do you live here?"

His English was really good, but that didn't mean he lived locally.

"I live nearby. Not far from here actually, over in Bellevue Hill. I've been in Australia since I was a young child."

She cocked her head at him. "Funny, considering how close you live, that I've not seen you around before."

"I don't normally attend markets. But I believe I've seen you on the beach before." He nodded at her hair. "You're rather distinctive."

She grinned. Her hair was purple with blue through it. It was a pain to maintain with all the time she spent in the water, but her best friend, Jess, was a hairdresser and gave her a very healthy discount. The bright mix of colours really did make her stand out.

"I'm down there most days giving surfing lessons. You should come down sometime. I'll be happy to give you a lesson or two."

Juli was proud of herself, being able to form complete, coherent sentences while she was nearly drooling at the thought of him shirtless in a pair of board shorts. A shudder ran through her as she imagined him wet on a board. And if she was teaching him, she would have to look. Rodger couldn't complain about that one. Well, he could, and no doubt *would* if he found out. She winced a little. Probably best if her fiancé didn't find out at all. If it ever happened, that is.

"Perhaps one day." His gaze went back to her photos, helping her to remember why she was here. She needed to sell something to him. It didn't matter if he was sex on a stick or looked like a hobo. Money was money, and she needed it.

"So, are you looking for something in particular?"

He ran his fingertip over the outside edge of the warehouse photo he'd been looking at earlier. It really was stunning, and with the colours of the setting sun behind the weather roughened exterior of the abandoned building, it had turned a completely average looking warehouse into something extraordinary.

"This one is exactly what I'm after."

She reached over with her left hand to pick up the photo, but he caught her hand and twisted it over to look at her fingers before she could pick it up. Tilting her hand, he ran his thumb over her engagement ring.

"Your man lets you catch a bus on your own?"

Frowning, she wriggled her fingers until he released her. She'd really prefer to not examine her relationship with Rodger too closely. She was rather scared of what she'd discover. Forcing her mind back on task, she picked up the image to wrap.

"We only have the one car, and he needs it for work." She shrugged. "It is what it is." At least he didn't work Sundays, so she had the car for the markets. It was depressing to think about exactly how little her fiancé seemed to care about her, with the way he was always putting himself and his needs above hers. It was another reason she did her best not to scrutinise her relationship with him too closely.

A low rumble came from the hot Russian.

"If you were my woman, you would never be left unprotected. He is not a real man if he leaves you open to attack like that."

She would definitely need to change her underwear when she got home. She was also in danger of swooning for real. This tall, dark, handsome sex god standing before her was a gentleman on top of everything else.

With a sad smile, she taped the tissue paper down and put the photo in a bag.

"Clearly, not all men are equal. Cash or card?"

She wanted this conversation over. This guy was a stranger. Hell, she didn't even know his name. She already knew Rodger wasn't the best bloke out there. Truthfully, lately she'd been thinking he was way closer to being one of the worst. But he was all she had, and she'd been stupid enough to say yes to his proposal, so now it looked like she'd be stuck with him forever. It was best if she tried not to think about it too much.

At least he didn't knock her around.

CHAPTER TWO

TWO MONTHS LATER

After she finished with her lessons for the afternoon, Juli wasn't ready to go home. For the last six weeks, she'd lived in a house with three other women. Two were backpackers who barely spoke English, and right now, she just didn't have the energy to deal with them. Jess, her best friend, lived there too, which was how Juli had come to live there. She'd already thought her friend was pretty awesome before she'd given her somewhere safe to land. But the way she'd helped Juli out had solidified the fact. Her bestie hadn't batted an eyelash when Juli had rocked up on the doorstep, black eye and all, to ask if she could stay with her.

Well, okay, that wasn't the complete truth. Jess had dragged her in and given her an ice pack for her face. After demanding Juli tell her what happened, Jess had been furious. She'd suggested all sorts of ways they could get some vengeance on Rodger. Seemed Jess didn't like the fact Rodger had beaten her up any more than she did. But when it came to giving her a safe place to land, Jess hadn't hesitated. Lucky for Juli, Jess had an empty room as one of the backpackers who'd been staying there had gone home the week before, and she hadn't gotten around to advertising the room yet.

The house was small but funky, and Juli actually really liked living there. It'd just be nice if it wasn't quite so crowded all the time. Maybe once she got herself out of debt, she'd suggest to Jess that they keep it to just the two of them. If only she wasn't paying off all the shit Rodger had run up in her name, she would have more money to put toward her living arrangements.

Having stored and locked up her surfing stuff, she then wandered around the streets of Bondi with her camera, looking for interesting shots. She needed some new, fresh images for her market stall. She had a mix of customers, both locals and tourists, but it was the tourists who generally bought up big, and they wanted unique views of the local landmarks.

With that in mind, she headed back down to the beach as the sun set. Her pulse jumped when she saw how the colours reflected on the clouds behind the Surf Lifesavers' tower. Now that would be a money shot. It would have been better if she could get the ocean in the background, but annoyingly, the sun set in the west so she had to make do with taking shots angled up so the image would only show the sky and the tower.

She quickly lifted her camera and snapped several photos, not wanting to lose the perfect lighting. She ended up staying there until well after the sun dipped below the horizon. The sky had really put on a show with different colours tonight, and she'd caught them all. With a wide grin, she made her way over the sand and back onto the roadway. Her new home was only two blocks from the main beach at Bondi, and over the past six weeks, she'd gotten used to walking the short distance. As she made her way down the footpath, she packed her camera up and zipped it safely away in its case before she tucked it in her large handbag.

With a sigh and a deep breath, she turned her attention to her surroundings. The bars and clubs were just starting to get busy while all the shops that were packed with tourists during the day now sat empty. She passed by a bar and shook her head with a chuckle when a wolf whistle rung out. *Men.* She didn't even consider stopping in for a drink. After the nightmare Rodger turned out to be, she had zero interest in men or relationships. Especially some bloke in a bar who thought whistling at a girl was a good way to get her attention.

Nope, she was going to work hard, save her money, and build a life for herself. Never again would she be stupid enough to fall for a man who wanted to move in together and combine incomes within weeks of meeting. In hindsight, there'd been so many warning signs that Rodger wasn't a good man. *Ah, well, live and learn.* She'd be a lot more careful in the future. Because, it turned out, all Rodger had wanted was access to her money, while making sure she had nowhere to go if she decided to leave. Jess was the only friend she had left, and because they mainly caught up when she went to get her hair done, Rodger obviously hadn't realised it. Also, he hadn't realised that physical violence was a deal breaker for her. Even if she'd ended up on the street for a night or two, she would never sit and take a man using her as a punching bag. *No, siree. Not ever.*

Lost in her thoughts, she wasn't aware she was in trouble until it was too late. A man was walking toward her, holding her gaze. She went to turn to head back to the more populated area of Bondi but came up short when a second man stood in her way.

"Whatcha doin', pretty lady?"

Looked like a couple of the men in that last bar had decided to follow her. Maybe she should have stopped in for that drink after all. She ran her gaze over the two men. They both looked like they spent a lot of time inside a gym. *Dammit.*

"Just heading home. I don't want any trouble. How about you both just go back into the bar and find some chick who's willing?"

As Juli predicted, they didn't take her suggestion. Nope, the bastards came in closer to her, forcing her to back up. A quick glance up and down the street showed her she was alone. It also showed her that these arseholes had followed her long enough she could barely hear the noise from the main road. No one out in the bars and clubs would hear her scream, that was for sure.

Bugger.

With a growl, Daniil frowned at the two men who'd just slipped from their stools and left the bar. He hoped he'd misread their intent, but he doubted it. His little purple-haired surfing photographer had strolled past a few moments earlier. He really should have asked her name when he'd bought that photo from her two months ago. He'd seen her many times since but had always stayed far enough away no one would realise he was watching her. Including the woman herself.

Like tonight, he'd seen her down on the beach taking photos of the tower. After observing her work for far too long, he'd come up here to one of the many bars to get a drink and perhaps relax a little. His obsession with this girl was strange, and way outside normal for him. He'd never felt the need to keep watch over a woman before. In fact, he couldn't recall an occasion when he'd put this much time into observing anyone. At least, not someone that wasn't related to a job. He knew his behaviour bordered on stalking. However, he couldn't seem to stop. It also didn't help that trouble seemed to follow her. Just last week he'd had to scare off a would-be-attacker when she'd been taking photos down the coast. The woman seriously needed a keeper. He honestly couldn't understand how she'd managed to survive this long in the world and remain so naive and, well, sweet. She was special, no doubt.

That was why he couldn't claim her for himself. She was all things bright and sunny in the world, while he lived in the darkness of the shadows. He'd never minded before, but over these past two months he'd begun to wonder what it would be like to have a woman of his own. Maybe even a family. But that would give him a major weakness that would leave him vulnerable. He shook his head. No, he would simply continue to guard her from a distance when he could.

Downing the last of his drink, he moved from his place at the bar and headed in the direction the men had gone. Apparently, his night was going to end with a little wet work, because if those two arseholes were going to make a try for his little surfer, he would intervene and make sure they were unable to ever try anything like it again.

He was far enough behind them he easily blended into the shadows to follow them past the bars and into the quieter back streets. Daniil shook his head as the woman strolled along, oblivious to the danger prowling after her. Where was her fiancé? He couldn't understand how any man who had a woman as pretty as her would ever let her out of his sight, let alone out in the night with no protection. Yet, all the times he'd seen her or followed her, he'd never once seen her with a man. Perhaps she had left him, or he her. Although he doubted the latter. Daniil had been tempted many times to dig deeper to obtain more information on her, but that would raise flags and put her in too much danger. Unless he was willing to claim her and put a guard on her around the clock, he couldn't afford the fact she held his attention to be known.

She turned down a side street, and while one man followed her, the other crossed the road and jogged down the opposite side before returning to her side of the road and coming back toward her. Daniil was still a distance behind them and knew he needed to quicken his pace if he wanted to prevent her from coming to any harm. Before he did, he pulled out his phone and sent a message to his most trusted associate, his right-hand man and close friend, Viktor, telling the man his location and that he'd need a pickup ASAP. When the return message came back with an ETA of five minutes, he picked up his pace as much as he could while remaining hidden in the shadows. When the men cornered her and herded her out of sight, Daniil broke free of the shadows and ran on silent feet. As he moved, he decided against pulling out his gun. Even with a silencer, a gunshot would still draw attention if he was forced to fire, so instead he palmed his knife from its holster and hoped he could get the job done using only that. Fortunately, he'd been working earlier, so he had the weapons on him. Australian gun laws were tight and didn't allow civilians to carry handguns around in public, so he didn't risk carrying often, but today's job had required it, and since he hadn't been home yet, he still had his equipment on him.

When he got within feet of where the trio had disappeared, he stepped back into the shadows but didn't stop moving forward. He could hear her sweet voice laced with fear, along with the gravelly, cocky voices of her would-be attackers. He slipped around the corner and barely held in his growl. One man had her held against his chest with an arm banded around her torso, holding her arms in against her body, while his other palm was over her mouth. Tears glistened in her eyes, and her chest rose and fell rapidly. She was panicking, with good reason. The bastard holding her was whispering in her ear, while the other arsehole came at her with a knife, holding the thing up to make sure she saw it. Her eyes were wide, and her gaze was focused solely on that blade.

In the seconds it took Daniil to plan his

attack to take them out, the arsehole slipped the blade under the centre of her bikini top and sliced through the material. Her whimper cut through Daniil like a whip. With his teeth bared, he stepped up behind the man holding the knife. Within seconds, he thrust his own blade into the neck of the bastard, severing his carotid artery. Blood gushed, and with a shocked gurgle, the man dropped his weapon in order to grab at his neck. It was human nature to try to stop the bleeding, but there was no way would the man survive the wound. Daniil was well trained in these matters and knew what he was doing.

He roughly shoved the dying man aside. He was no longer the active threat, so Daniil moved on to the man who was. As the bastard pulled his head back from her ear in shock, Daniil switched his hold on the knife and threw it. His aim was true, and the blade slid easily into the man's eye. She stumbled as the man fell, but Daniil didn't let her go down. He snatched her to him, her palms and bare breasts pressed against his chest. Her sweet citrus scent mixed with the smell of the ocean had a shudder running through his body. Damn, but she was beyond beautiful, and he was struggling to restrain his cock's reaction to her close proximity.

"You are safe now, *krasivaya*."

She blinked up at him with a vacant look in her eyes before her pupils rolled back and she went limp against him. Not wanting Viktor to see her topless when he arrived, Daniil awkwardly shrugged out of his jacket and wrapped it around her.

"Ah, *solnyshka moto*, this is going to change everything."

This wasn't a job, and him helping a random stranger without reason was unheard of. Everyone in his employ would hear about this before daybreak. And as much as he trusted those closest to him, people talked, and soon a friend of a friend would tell someone who wanted him harmed that he now had a weakness they could exploit.

Viktor pulled up, and Daniil swung her up in his arms and headed toward the vehicle. He laid her over the rear seat before heading back to help Viktor bag up the bodies.

Once they had them stored in the rear of

the van, Daniil snatched up her bag from the ground and headed back to her. He climbed into the rear and lifted her head so it rested against his thigh. Even with her unconscious, his dick twitched to life at having her so near.

Bloody hell, this woman was going to be trouble. He knew it.

He started going through her bag, looking for her purse and driver's licence. Since all his good intentions had gone to hell, he may as well take the opportunity to find out a little about her.

Things like her name.

CHAPTER THREE

A gentle touch down her cheek had Juli stirring awake. With a groan, she rolled to her side, blinking her eyes clear.

"What the hell?"

With a jerk, she shifted across the bed, away from the sexy Russian man she'd met at the markets a couple of months ago. He was lying beside her, attired in dark dress pants and a tight black T-shirt that hugged his muscular torso like a glove. Stretched out on his side facing her, he looked like some kind of sleek predator. *A panther.* That's what he made her think of when she saw him. Sleek and beautiful, but dangerous.

"Relax, *krasivaya.* You're safe here with me."

With a frown, she tore her gaze away

from him and glanced around, but she couldn't see much. The only light was from a bedside lamp set on low, and that only revealed the large bed they were on. The fact she couldn't see any walls aside from the one behind the bed had her thinking it was a large room.

"Where is *here* exactly?"

"My home. Do you remember what happened?"

Memories flashed through her mind as she thought back. Memories of the two men cornering her, grabbing her, then him appearing out of nowhere and ... that was the last thing she remembered. Raising a palm to rub her eyes, she realised she was wearing a jacket. She focused on her arms, then her chest. Was she wearing his clothes? She pressed her nose to the collar and inhaled. It smelled like him, so yep, this was definitely her Russian's suit coat. That crisp, fresh, slightly spicy scent she'd not been able to get out of her head for days after he'd bought that photo from her.

"I remember the men grabbing me, and you arriving. But nothing after that."

He made a noise in the back of his throat

that had her gaze flicking up to his. He looked happy with the fact she couldn't remember. She sure as hell wasn't impressed with her memory blank spot.

"Tell me what happened, and why am I wearing your jacket? Please."

He frowned and reached his hand over to tuck some loose strands of her hair behind her ear. She'd put it up in her usual twin braids this morning, but by the end of the day there were always sections that came loose and hung around her face. A shiver ran over her body when his callused fingers stroked her cheek as he pulled back. Yep, this guy was seriously dangerous to a woman's sanity.

"All you need to know is that I took care of them in a way that assures they won't bother you again. And you're wearing my jacket because those bastards cut your top."

His fist clenched on the bed between them. Instinctively wanting to soothe him, she reached over and covered his hand with her palm. A moment later, he unclenched his fist before he moved to slide his fingers between hers, curling them to keep their hands joined.

"Thank you. You don't even know me, had no reason to get involved, but you did, and I'm extremely grateful. How did you find me?"

She remembered the men herding her into a little laneway, out of sight from the road.

"I was having a drink in the same bar as them. I recognised your hair as you walked past. So, when I saw those two arseholes take off to follow you after they'd been talking about you, I followed them. You've been on my mind since you sold me that photo, and I didn't want to see you come to harm."

He was frowning as though he wasn't entirely happy about the fact that he'd saved her. She didn't like the idea he regretted his actions. Juli certainly didn't. She gave him a soft smile.

"Well, I'm really grateful you did whatever you did. And I hadn't forgotten about you either."

His blue gaze snapped up to hers.

"Truth?"

She chuckled. "Which part? That I'm

thankful you saved my arse, or that I've thought of you since the markets?"

He growled low before he released her hand and moved in. Like the panther she'd labelled him earlier, he prowled with sleek, powerful movements until he had her pinned beneath him. She gasped out a shocked breath at how fast he'd moved. Then a shiver ran through her at how good it felt to be caged beneath his muscular frame, surrounded by his scent. He held his weight mostly on his arms, his bicep muscles bulging with the strain.

Unable to resist the temptation, she ran her palms over the smooth, inked skin of his arms, following the lines of his muscles. With another growl, he lowered his face in close to her neck, inhaling against her skin before he lightly nipped at her throat, making her shiver.

"You are not wearing your ring, *krasivaya*. Does that mean you're now single?"

She stiffened at the reminder of her ex. Of the violent backhand he'd given her the day she'd left him. On reflex, she cringed away from him, pushing herself into the soft mattress. He lifted up on his arms, giving her a little space.

"Are you not single? Tell me."

She winced. Bugger. He must think she was pulling away out of guilt. "I'm single. I left my ex over a month ago."

"Why did you flinch when I asked about him? What did he do to you?"

She shook her head. "I don't want to think about him. Please." She lifted her palms to cup his face, his neatly trimmed steel grey beard soft against her skin. She was well aware she was being reckless as hell, allowing her body to make decisions it shouldn't. But she didn't care. He was being nice to her, acting like he gave a damn about her. She'd had so little of that throughout her life, and she wanted to bask in it while she could. "Kiss me?"

His gaze stayed hard for a moment before it began to melt into something softer, sexier.

"You *will* tell me later what happened that made you flinch at the thought of him."

Before she could respond, he lowered his mouth to hers. His lips were soft yet commanding, and he stole her breath as he proceeded to kiss her passionately. The arousal that raced through her blood cleared her mind of all other thoughts.

Tilting his head, Daniil kissed his Julietta deeper. She was like his very own personal brand of cocaine. While he'd never seen the point of taking drugs that would remove his control over himself, he couldn't resist her. One taste and he was hooked. So much so, that it wiped his mind of all other thoughts except for one. The fact he'd noticed some bruising on her face around the time she said she left her ex. He'd assumed it had been a surfing accident, and from a distance, he hadn't even been certain it was a bruise and not just shadows over her face. It was something he planned on getting to the bottom of later. If her ex had laid a hand on his Julietta, the man would pay for it. But not right now. Right now, he was busy enjoying the woman who'd occupied his thoughts far too fully for far too long. He shifted so his weight was on one arm, freeing up the other to cup her face with his palm. Her cheek was like silk against his skin, and he needed to feel more of her.

It hadn't been the time or place earlier for him to check out her breasts. His need to cover her before Viktor arrived had been more important than checking out her assets. But now was a different story. She was squirming and moaning beneath him as he continued to kiss her.

He slid his hand under her back before he rolled them over, so she was now on top of him. Pressing her palms on his pecs, she broke the kiss to sit up. Her legs had fallen on either side of his hips, which left his rock-hard cock up against her pussy. Even through their clothes, the heat of her scorched him as though they were naked.

With a groan, he gripped her hips and thrust up against her a few times.

"I want you, Julietta. You going to let me take you?"

He wasn't sure what he'd do if she said no. He'd never rape a woman, of course, but he may just perish from the pain of blue balls if she made him stop at this point.

Stilling, she frowned. "How do you know my name?"

That left him wincing as he hoped this didn't ruin the moment. "After you passed out, I looked through your bag to find your I.D. I wanted to be sure you didn't have any sort of medical condition I needed to be aware of."

That hadn't been his reason for looking, but it was a valid point that he hoped would have her giving him a pass on invading her privacy.

"Ah, okay. Well, no one calls me Julietta. It's just Juli."

He grinned at her, flexing his fingers against her hips. "Well, I'll be calling you Julietta. I like how it rolls off my tongue. Now, you need to answer my question. Will you let me have you?"

She gave him a small smile as she nodded slightly. "Yes." Then she sat up straight and began to slip open the buttons on his jacket. He loved how she looked wearing his clothing. It was way too big for her and made her look feminine, fragile, and like she was his woman. As the black material slipped from her shoulders, her perky tits were bared to him, their tight peaks making him growl as a new wave of desire flowed through him. She wasn't as well-endowed as some of his past lovers, but he didn't care. She was all natural and plenty big enough to fill his palms and then some. He'd fucked more than a few Barbie-doll type women, who had surgically altered their bodies to what they thought men wanted. He couldn't speak for all men, but for him, natural beauty would always shine brighter than anything made of silicone and plastic. Especially when the natural beauty was confident in herself, which his little surfer was.

"*Ti kraslvaya.*" He shook his head a little before translating his words when she frowned at him. "You are lovely."

Despite being raised in Australia since he'd been a young boy, Daniil had tried to keep at least a few of his native Russian words in his vocabulary. Not so many that he would constantly need to explain himself to people, but he found the odd curse word or endearment spoken in his native tongue was enough to settle his heart that he was staying true to his heritage. Didn't hurt that women seemed to swoon at his accent and whispered Russian words.

He sat up, and with a palm behind her back, arched her toward him as he wrapped his lips around one of her dusty-pink nipples. The peak not in his mouth, he teased with his other hand, pulling and tugging on her nipple with his finger and thumb as he nipped, licked and tormented the other with his mouth. She tasted so sweet, with an edge of saltiness from the ocean, and he knew instantly he'd never get enough of her.

As she ground her pelvis against his, she used both hands in his hair to hold him against her, not that he had any intention of going anywhere. His cock was about to burst through his pants to get to her, he was that desperate for her. He rolled them again, and sitting back in a kneel, he pulled her shorts and panties down her long, lean legs. Tossing the clothing on the floor with one hand, he kept her foot in his other. He reached over to turn the lamp to a brighter setting before he pressed a kiss to the arch of her foot while he ran his gaze over her now naked form in the brighter light.

She squirmed on the mattress as he took her in. She was glorious. The paler skin around her waist and breasts drew his attention. He grinned at the thought of him convincing her to try sunbathing naked to even out her tan. He could just imagine how stunning she would look with the bright sunshine on her skin. Her pussy was waxed bare, and he licked his lips as he noticed the glistening of moisture on her folds. He was desperate for a taste of her cream. Would it be as sweet as her skin?

He pressed kisses up the inside of her leg and nipped her inner thigh when she tried to pull her legs closed. With a gasp at his nip, her muscles loosened enough he could make more room for himself between her thighs. He pressed his nose into the crease between her leg and torso, inhaling her musk. He felt animalistic around this woman, to the point he barely resisted the urge to mark her like some kind of beast would his mate. He had *never* felt like this, and if he wasn't half mad with desire, he probably would have freaked the fuck out. But too much of his blood had pooled in his dick to give his brain enough to function correctly, because he wasn't worried. Not one bit. He shifted his mouth over and ran his tongue slowly through her folds, collecting her honey and enjoying the hell out of the way she shuddered beneath him.

He pulled back slightly to savour her unique flavour. "Damn, you taste so good. But I need more."

She didn't say a word, just continued to pant as he fastened his mouth back over her pussy and ate at her like she was the most decadent food he'd ever tasted. Because she was. Moving up to suckle on her hard, little clit, he thrust two fingers inside her wet channel. He stroked and searched until he found the spot deep within her that made her cry out, and then with a wicked grin, he set about driving her insane.

In a matter of minutes, he had her thrashing on the mattress, and then she came and gave him more of her sweet cream. He couldn't get enough of her and only allowed her a few moments to settle before he began working his fingers within her again. He needed more of her taste down his throat.

"Again, *krasivaya*. Come for me again."

She groaned, but he didn't give her time to form words before he fastened his lips over her clit and tormented the little nub with his tongue and teeth. Not only did he want to drink down more of her sweet honey, but he needed her relaxed enough to take his size. He knew he was a large man, and he wanted her so badly, he was going to struggle to not simply thrust deep into her tight, little body on his first stroke.

CHAPTER FOUR

Never had Juli had a lover with such exceptional oral skills. If she died right now, she'd go happy. As she floated down from her second massive climax, she lay limp on the bed, watching him. While he'd stripped her down to her skin, he was still completely dressed. Somehow, that made the experience even hotter. The fact he wanted her so much had her heart skipping a beat.

Through hooded eyes, she didn't look away as he slipped from the bed and began stripping. She may have even started drooling when he casually reached behind himself, gripped the back of his shirt and pulled it over his head. That had to be the single most masculine way possible of taking off a shirt. His chest was smoothly muscled, and while not bulky, he was clearly strong. The tattoos that ran up his arms weren't the only ones he had. His upper chest also had ink. Then he unbuttoned his pants, and she forgot all about his tattoos.

The black material of his suit pants hadn't given her much of an idea as to what was underneath, although what he'd pressed against her earlier had felt sizeable. He slipped his thumbs under the waistband and shoved both his pants and boxers down his legs in one fast move.

"Oh, fuck."

The curse slipped out before she could stop it. He chuckled darkly, and she started to rub her legs together as another wave of arousal along with a little fear ran through her bloodstream. He was very well endowed. Like, bigger than any man she'd ever taken inside her before. With another of his insanely sexy growls, he knelt on the bed then prowled toward her until he once more had her caged beneath him. The heat he radiated had her trembling and arching up, trying to get closer to his warmth. He lowered his body down until the hard planes of his chest pressed against her peaked nipples. She wrapped her legs around his, tilting her hips to rub against his thick length that lay over her mound.

"You like what you see, *krasivaya*?"

She moaned as she shifted her hips, trying desperately to get his cock inside her. He had her so turned on, she could barely think.

"Need you so bad. Please, stop teasing!"

He gave her an evil-looking smirk. "Ah, but teasing is all part of the fun."

He reached over her and opened the drawer on the bedside table. This left his nipple right in front of her mouth, so she nuzzled then licked at it. The way he sucked in a breath gave her the courage she needed to keep going, and she gently bit the tight little bud, giving it a small tug before she released it.

In a fast, smooth motion, he moved until his face was level with hers. He took her mouth with a passion that bordered on desperation. He groaned and rubbed his thick erection against her mound, coating his dick with her arousal as he slid his length against her folds. She arched her hips, trying again to get him to thrust inside her. Her body was on fire for this man.

He pulled back with another growl, and she whimpered at the loss. The crinkle of foil had her smiling. *Condom.* She hadn't even thought of it. She was on the pill so no risk there, and while she was clean, she had no idea if he was. Hell, she didn't even know his name! That thought had her frowning. She probably should have asked that already. The sight of him running his big hand over his even bigger cock had her tongue briefly sticking to the roof of her mouth, halting the question for a moment longer.

"What's your name?"

He paused in his movements to raise an eyebrow at her.

"Daniil." He smirked at her. "I look forward to hearing you screaming it shortly."

He ran his fingers through her soaked folds before he lined up the head of his dick with her entrance.

"You ready for me, Julietta?"

He rubbed his cockhead through her folds again and her desperation for him grew.

"Fuck, yes! Stop teasing me already!"

The gleam in his eye made her pause. Maybe she shouldn't have pushed him to hurry up. Before she could try to backtrack, he slammed that huge dick of his inside her on one stroke, and she screamed as her back arched and her body spasmed while it adjusted to the invasion. Daniil's body trembled above her as he held still within her, but he didn't thrust again until after she managed to take a deep inhale and began to grind against him.

"So tight. So good." He growled the words as he pulled out then slid back in. With each stroke, he touched nerves Juli hadn't known she had. He filled her completely, and with each thrust he bumped against her cervix, the small bite of pain sending her arousal spiralling higher.

She ran her palms up his muscular arms, over his shoulders then up into his hair. Needing more of his kisses, she used her hands to guide his face down to hers. He flashed her a cocky grin before giving in to her silent demand. He slowed his thrusts as he took her mouth to kiss her deeply, melting her beneath him. Then he tore his lips from hers and rose to kneel between her thighs.

Before she could catch her breath, he took a firm grip on her hips and began fucking her hard and fast. He moved his thumb to tweak her clit with each stroke, and she didn't stand a chance. She blew apart, screaming his name loud enough she was sure the entire suburb knew what they were doing.

Not that she cared.

Daniil growled again then held still, his cock jerking within her as he came. With a shudder, he fell forward over her, giving her his full weight for the first time, and she basked in how he made her feel grounded. Wrapping her arms around him, she held tight, keeping him close in an attempt to hold on to her bliss. Moments later, he moved his head to press a kiss to her throat before he pulled back. A pang hit her heart when she realised she wasn't strong enough to prevent him from leaving her.

"Let me clean up. I'll be right back."

Reluctantly she lowered her arms, freeing him fully. She arched with a moan as his dick slid free from her pussy. She was going to be feeling him for a while. His hot, wet mouth covered her nipple for a moment, tormenting her until she was squirming and reaching to pull him back over her.

With a chuckle, he rolled from the bed before she could stop him and walked away. Her gaze caught on his arse and stayed there until he ducked into another room and out of sight. Damn, he was one well put together man, that was for sure. Her body was sore, but his teasing her before he left had her wanting more. *Dammit.* She'd never been this insatiable before in her life! Normally, one orgasm and she was ready for a sleep. He'd given her how many now? Three, four? And she still wanted more.

♛

With a shake of his head, he removed the condom from his dick, then tossed it in the bin before he moved to the sink to wash his hands and wet a cloth. He wiped himself over quickly before rinsing out the cloth with warm water to take to Julietta. She was a little firecracker, that was for sure. Thinking of how her body came back to life as he'd teased her breast had his cock growing hard again. Would she be ready for another round so soon? She'd been tight around him, and he knew she'd no doubt be sore tomorrow, but he hoped tonight she'd be willing to let him have her a few more times. He'd make sure any discomfort she felt in the morning would be well worth it.

He strode back into the bedroom but stopped short at the sight that greeted him. A breath hissed in through his teeth as he took in his Julietta. Like some kind of wet dream, she was spread across his bed, one hand between her thighs, two of her slender fingers deep within her pussy while her other hand tugged at the nipple he'd had his mouth on just a few minutes ago.

He wanted to film her like this, so he could watch it over and over again. Before he could think better of it, he silently grabbed his phone from the table near him. She hadn't noticed that he'd returned to the room yet, so with the press of a few buttons he took a couple photos and a short video, all while he used his free hand to tug his cock in time to her fingers thrusting in and out of her slick pussy.

With her eyes still closed, she arched her back and groaned as she came. A tiny climax compared to the ones she'd had earlier with him, but it was still sexy as hell to watch her experience it. He turned off the video, happy with what he'd captured of her, and slid the phone back onto the table. He'd make sure she never knew he had it, and no one would ever see it, other than him, of course. He was going to be watching it often, he was sure.

He moved on silent feet until he stood beside the bed.

"Do you need more, *krasivaya*?"

Her cheeks pinkened, and with a gasp, she jerked her hands away from her body. Daniil set the cloth on the bedside table and reached for another condom to suit up. Despite the fact he was well into his forties now, he still had a reputation for his stamina, and by morning, she'd know how true it was. Gripping her ankles, he pulled her to the edge of the mattress before moving his hands up to her hips to help her roll over onto her belly. Then he guided her up until she was on her hands and knees with her delectable arse in the air in front of him. Taking his cock in hand, he teased her slick entrance with the head for a second before he thrust deep into her tight, wet heat. When he bottomed out, her channel rippled around him. He dug his fingers into her hips as she stole his breath for a few moments.

"You truly are glorious."

He leaned forward and, running a palm up her front, lifted her so her back was against his chest as he straightened to stand behind her. He bit her shoulder, sucking on her skin to leave his mark there as he began to thrust his hips. She whispered his name, whimpered, then threw her head back against his shoulder as he lifted his mouth from her and continued to fuck her. Moving his palm to between her thighs, he began to tease her clit as he maintained his strong thrusts into her. He knew she'd be sensitive by this point, but the way she tightened around him when she came was too good to resist doing all he had to in order to feel it again.

"Play with your breasts. Tug on those pretty nipples for me."

He nipped her ear after whispering his commands, and with a shudder, she slowly raised her hands to do as he'd asked. The sight of her tugging and twisting her tight little peaks as he worked her clit and thrust his cock in deep, pushed him close to the edge. She moved her hips with him, letting him know she was fully in the moment with him, enjoying their fucking as much as he was. He couldn't believe his good fortune that he had finally found his match. Not many women could keep up with his sexual appetite, but his Julietta seemed to thrive on it. Time would tell if she was truly up for the challenge of being his lover, or if this was just because she'd had a near death experience and was looking for something to shock her back into reality.

He was certain by morning he'd know which it was, because neither he nor Julietta would be getting much sleep tonight, that was for sure. She tightened around him again, ending all his other thoughts. She cried out his name as she came and bathed his cock in a fresh wave of her heat. He rapidly thrust into her several more times before allowing himself to go over the edge, filling the condom once more.

Wrapping his arms around her, he held her against him, not wanting to leave her body. She leaned her full weight back against him, and he stroked the sweaty skin of her flat stomach and rounded breasts with his palms.

"You're insatiable."

He kissed the side of her throat, grinning at her words. "Only when I have a beautiful, willing woman in my bed."

After another minute of stroking her, and of her clenching down on his rapidly hardening cock, he pulled free of her and threw her over his shoulder. She shrieked as she landed, and he slapped her arse as he laughed.

"Shower time, *krasivaya*. Then I'll dirty you up again."

He couldn't wait to have her all slick and wet against him. He hoped she liked shower sex. And he needed to find out if she was on birth control. At the rate they were going, he was going to run out of condoms quickly, and way before he'd had his fill of her.

CHAPTER FIVE

With her heart pounding in her chest, Juli woke with a start. Memories of last night flashed through her mind. The two men attacking her, before the Russian dude from the markets appeared out of nowhere and saved her. After passing out, she'd woken to find herself in his bed, and things had rapidly heated up. *Had they ever.* She and her Russian, Daniil, had sex. Lots and lots of spectacular sex. After scrubbing her hands over her face, she blinked her eyes clear. She was still in his bed, but now it was morning. Rays of light came from around the closed blinds to reveal the room. The elegant grey and white sheets over her were nothing like the bright colours she had on her own bed. Holy shit, she'd been right about the room being big. Actually, that was an understatement. She sat up to take in the massive space. Pale sandstone walls and pristine honey-coloured polished timber floors, along with the sparce decorations around the room, made it look like some kind of display home for the rich and famous.

Taking a deep breath, she shored up her courage and turned to look at the other half of the bed. Her breath caught at the sight Daniil made, lying there with the sheet down around his waist. While she'd thought he looked hot in the black shirt and pants he'd worn to the markets, he was devastating with no clothes on. Her lips quirked when she noticed that, even in rest, his face looked strong and harsh, as though he couldn't fully relax.

As he was lying on his back, she could see all the tattoos she'd caught glimpses of last night. Her gaze trailed over his pecs and the large black ink tattoos that covered them. Curiosity had her making a mental note to ask him about the meaning behind them all, and why he had no colour in any of his ink.

With a frown, she closed her eyes. What

was she doing? There would be no later conversations. She didn't want a man! Any man. She was going to rock being Miss Independent for the rest of her days, no matter how good-looking or how fantastic at sex the man was.

At the thought of having sex with him, her pussy came awake. Dammit, she shouldn't want sex for a month after last night, yet her body knew who was lying next to her and wanted more of what they'd done overnight. How many times had he taken her? She'd stopped even attempting to keep count after their hot and steamy shower. Speaking of the bathroom, her full bladder was demanding attention.

She slipped from the bed and padded over the smooth floorboards toward the bathroom. She'd barely seen it last night. Daniil had kept her very busy and completely focused on him when he'd brought her in here for their shower. She flipped a switch, and with a gasp, she clung to the door frame. Bathroom didn't seem like the right word to describe this room. It was bigger than her bedroom at the shared house, and by the looks of it, constructed entirely from marble.

With another deep breath, she forced her feet to cross the floor toward the toilet. Once she did her thing, she washed her hands and looked at herself in the mirror. She'd put her hair in two braids yesterday morning as she normally did, but they were now all but destroyed. Between getting them wet in the shower, then all the action on the bed, she wasn't surprised. She tugged the hair ties out and began to finger comb through the tangles the best she could. She fortunately rarely wore makeup, so her face was as fresh and clean as always, but her body was a different story. A large love bite marked her shoulder, and several other smaller bites were scattered over her chest and torso. Bugger. It looked like she'd be wearing a shirt over her bikini for the next few days.

A knock on the door had her jumping with a squeal.

"*Solnyshka moto*. Sorry, Julietta, I didn't mean to startle you. Are you all right?"

She spun to see him leaning against the door frame, looking way too sexy for his own good. He'd not bothered with clothes, and his dick was thick and hard, pointing toward her like it was trying to show Daniil where he needed to go. Her tongue stuck to the roof of her mouth as her gaze followed a ripple of movement over his chest and abs.

"Um, what happened last night?"

She needed to focus, dammit. She forced her gaze up to his face. His blue eyes were hard as he frowned at her. "You don't remember what we did?"

Like she'd ever forget the way that man could move between the sheets.

"I remember *that*. In fact, I can remember everything except for the part where you 'dealt with' my attackers. I need to report them to the police, and they need to pay for what they tried to do to me."

He nodded slowly as he ran a hand through his steel grey hair. Her fingers twitched at the memory of running through it last night. Her gaze dropped when the flex of his abdominal muscles again caught her attention.

"I took care of them. That's all you need to know. The police don't need to be told anything. I promise, they won't ever bother you again."

She frowned up at him. He sounded pretty damn sure of himself, which had her even more curious about how he'd handled them. "What did you do?"

He shook his head. "*Krasivaya*, it's nothing you need to worry about."

He kept calling her that, and she hated not knowing what it meant. "What does that mean? *Krasivaya*."

"Beautiful. It's a Russian endearment."

She nodded as her ovaries threatened to explode. He thought she was beautiful. Of course, he was also most likely a criminal who'd done something horrible to those men last night. She licked her lips when the silence dragged on.

"I don't suppose you could give me a lift home?"

He frowned and his expression turned dark. Juli's palms began to sweat as fear tickled up her spine. Had he made the most of her situation last night to kidnap her? To keep her locked up here as some sort of personal sex slave? She backed away from him but had nowhere to go. When her butt hit the cold marble wall, she was reminded that she was as naked as he was. Her gaze darted around the room, but there was no other door, aside from the one he was blocking.

"Please don't hurt me. I just want—"

A low growl cut off her words and left her cringing and whimpering.

"I will *never* harm you, Julietta. You have no need to ever fear me."

Yeah, that's easier said than done.

He prowled into the room toward her and suddenly, all those sexy muscles took on new meaning. He could hurt her easily if he wanted to.

"Then why can't I go home?"

"Because I still have plans for you."

Throughout his life, Daniil had strived to strike fear into many people. However, Julietta was not one of them. He hated that she was cowering in his bathroom, naked and afraid of what he was planning to do with her. He moved to stand in front of her, pausing before he reached for her. Her breath hitched and her body stiffened as he cupped her cheek in his palm.

"*Solnyshka moto*, I vow to you that you

need not fear me. Anyone who does hurt you is a different matter. But for you, I will always be a protector."

He sighed as emotions flitted over her face. He could tell she didn't believe him.

She cleared her throat. "I need to get to work."

He doubted that, but he nodded anyway. "It's still early. What time do you need to be there?"

While she now knew he'd looked through her bag to find her name, she didn't need to know he'd also searched her planner and had seen she was spending her afternoon at the hairdresser today. Closing her eyes, she leaned into his hand for a moment before, with a deep breath, she pulled away from his touch.

"Thank you for saving me last night, and for everything else. I had fun with you, but I need to go now."

A strange tightness filled his chest. Julietta was blowing him off after the night they'd shared. Was she insane? Although, she *had* been attacked last night. Honestly, he'd been surprised at how calm she was at waking to find herself in his bed. Maybe this was simply some kind of delayed reaction to her nearly being assaulted.

He couldn't believe what he was about to say. For the first time in his life, he didn't want to stick with his "only fuck them once" rule.

"I want to see you again."

Her eyes filled with moisture, but she didn't let any tears fall, just shook her head.

"I'm not looking for a boyfriend, Daniil. I just got free, and I don't want to get trapped again."

He couldn't hold back the wince. Would she feel trapped under his protection? It wouldn't be his intention, but he wasn't sure how she'd see it. She wasn't from his world, and didn't understand she'd need to be guarded like the jewel she was. Of course, after what he'd done for her last night, she'd find herself with protection now regardless of what she thought. Daniil would just have to make sure they knew to be careful not to let her see them as they kept her safe.

"This chemistry we have? I've never felt anything like it before, Julietta. I don't want to throw it away without seeing where it could go. What did your ex do to you that has you trying so hard to remain an island?"

She shuddered and sucked in a breath.

"I really wish you wouldn't ask so many questions. My ex hurt me. I trusted him, and he hurt me. He wasn't the first person in my life to do that, but I think it's time I try to limit who I let close enough to me to be able to cause me more pain."

What had his poor Julietta suffered through in her life to give her such an outlook? He didn't think she was simply scared of letting him close and him breaking her heart. At least she wasn't *only* afraid for her heart. She didn't need to be, as that's not how men in his family worked. Some might say they barely knew each other, but the way they fit together, the off-the-charts chemistry? That all told Daniil that she was his special one, and he had no intention of letting her get away from him. He could hardly believe how much his mindset had changed since he'd first met this little purple-haired surfing photographer. Despite never wanting to settle down in the past, he now couldn't wait to do just that. But only with her.

"Okay, how about you take a shower while I get us some breakfast sorted out? Then I'll drive you home."

She gave him a sad smile and nodded. Yeah, she didn't really want him to walk away any more than he wanted to leave. He cupped her face in his palms and kissed her deeply, letting her feel his desire for her.

"I'll grab one of my shirts for you to wear with your shorts before I head downstairs. Come find me when you're ready."

Despite it being the last thing he wanted to do, he forced himself to leave her. He grabbed one of his plain black T-shirts and brought it to her, along with her panties and shorts.

"Thank you."

With a smile he didn't feel, he left her alone in his bathroom. What he really wanted to do was to help wash her sexy little body and take her again in the shower. She'd been sexy as fuck last night, all wet and slippery against him. He sighed as he quickly dressed and headed downstairs. Not only did he need to put together breakfast, but he also needed to arrange a bodyguard for her before she finished in the shower.

His day was fully booked with work, so as much as he hated that Julietta was forcing him to release her, it was for the best. He couldn't afford to take the day off to spend it in bed fucking his girl. At least, not today. Although, he'd be making sure he could, and would, do exactly that very soon. He was looking forward to testing out which of them had more stamina. After last night, he wasn't sure who'd win.

CHAPTER SIX

Nearly a week later, Juli was busy setting up her stall at the Bondi markets.

"You really gonna keep turning him down?"

Jess had come to help her set up and, apparently, grill her about her Russian.

"After Rodger, I don't want another bloke. He was great between the sheets, but I'm not interested in getting tangled up with a man. Especially an older guy who will want to take control. I need to focus on getting my life back in order."

Thanks to Rodger, all her savings were now gone. She hadn't realised until after she walked out exactly how much that man had spent. Why had she ever agreed to give him access to her account? She mentally shook her head. She didn't want to think about him and his shit anymore. What she needed to do was knuckle down, start saving her money again, and get back on top of things.

"You know, with a guy like that Russian, you wouldn't have to worry about money ever again, babe. The fact he's older just means there's a higher chance he's got his shit together. And the way that guy dresses makes it clear he's not hurting for cash. You get that, right?"

Juli raised an eyebrow at her friend. They'd known each other since the start of high school, so Jess really should know her better than to suggest she'd be happy with some kind of sugar daddy.

"I'm not built that way. I can't just be some ... pampered pet to a rich man. No way. I'm my own person."

Jess was silent as she helped her set up the final stand.

"Some advice? Don't kick this guy to the kerb for another man's crimes. He's sent you flowers. Lots of really nice flowers. And all he wants is to take you out to dinner. You know he's good for it, so why not have some fun with him?"

Juli couldn't stop the grin that tugged at her mouth as she remembered what he'd done. On Wednesday afternoon, just after she'd arrived home from work, a delivery man rocked up with the biggest arrangement of flowers she'd ever seen. Naturally, it arrived in a freaking crystal vase. That vase was officially her most expensive possession.

Four days later, her room still smelt sweet, and with every breath she took of the scent, she thought of Daniil. Of his request for dinner. He'd wanted to take her out last night, but she'd turned him down. She was serious about getting back on her feet under her own steam. Full Miss Independent style was her new mantra. She'd made a mistake falling for Rodger and his shit, one she should have known better than to make. Had she learned nothing from her mother?

That soured her mood. Her mother hadn't had the best luck with men. Juli didn't know who her biological father was. If her mother had known, she'd never shared the information with her. And none of the string of men her mother latched onto during her childhood had exactly been stepfather material. Nope, right up until the day she ended her life, she was chasing the BBD (bigger, better deal) but never found it. A snort escaped Juli's throat. Her mother would have *loved* Daniil. Probably would have moved in with the guy already. But she wasn't her mother. No way. Juli had her pride and refused to follow in those particular footsteps. Rodger had been a harsh reminder of how easily a man could worm his way into her life and cause her pain.

"Men like Daniil, they don't do 'fun'. He's intense. So fucking intense. I know if I give him an inch, he'll take a mile."

Jess pulled her in for a hug. "Well, just think about it. Rodger is an arsehole, but not all men are. Hate to see you throw away a good one now just because you had bad luck with your ex."

Her friend walked away, leaving Juli with a headache forming from all the thoughts tripping over each other. Should she risk giving Daniil a chance? Was she being too stubborn for her own good? Even though she still wasn't sure exactly what Daniil had done to "deal with" her attackers, it had been nice to have him step up for her. When she'd woken up in his bed in his freaking huge mansion, she'd felt safe. Like somewhere deep inside, her inner cavewoman knew Daniil was capable of keeping her protected.

"Hey, babe."

An icy shiver ran down her spine at the sound of that deep voice. Rodger was the last person she wanted to deal with today. Shoring up her courage with a deep breath, she turned to face her ex with a glare.

"What the hell do you want?"

He had his most charming grin in full force and had dressed carefully in clean jeans and loose, button-up shirt. Daniil put him to shame in every way, and she wondered how she'd ever thought Rodger was worth her energy.

"What do you think? I miss you. I want to know when you're coming home."

She shook her head in disbelief. He was completely delusional.

"We broke up, Rodger, remember? It's over. Move on already."

He frowned at her, a flash of anger sparkling in his gaze, reminding her of the main reason why she'd never go back to this man. Not that she needed the reminder.

"One little fight doesn't change the fact you agreed to be my wife, Juli. You need to stop mucking around and come home where you belong."

She crossed her arms over her chest as her own anger rose.

"Little fight? You backhanded me hard enough to send me to the floor! And in that moment, you destroyed any chance you ever had of me being your wife."

Looking at him now, after being away from him for the past few months, she couldn't work out what she'd ever seen in him. He was pretty enough, with his dark, slicked-back hair and casually stylish clothes. But he also had a sleazy edge she'd not noticed before. How had she missed that?

He reached forward to grab her wrist, using it to pull her toward him.

"What are you doing? Let me go."

She tried to twist free of his grip, but he held firm, tugging her forward, around the table until she stood nearly touching him. She kept her body sideways, so it was only her shoulder and arm that made contact. The last thing she wanted was to have her breasts pressed against him. She needed to stop wearing bikinis all the time, because no matter how cool and comfortable they were on a hot summer's day, she was beginning to hate the way so many men thought they could touch her however they pleased when she wore one.

"I know you've been slutting around with that Russian bastard, but enough games. You. Are. Mine. Always will be. So, cut the bullshit and come home."

If she were a violent person, she'd sock him in the face for that comment. Inwardly, she sighed. Pity she wasn't a fighter. Maybe she should take some lessons. It seemed like a good thing to know, how to knock a bastard on his arse. Pulling her thoughts back to the present, she frowned his way.

"Have you lost your damn mind? I'm not yours, and I will never be. Not ever again."

With a sharp, fast movement, he twisted her hand up behind her, forcing her to lift on her toes with a gasp. Tears pricked her eyes at the pain that shot through her system. Yeah, maybe mouthing off and poking the crazy hadn't been the best idea. But they were in a public place, dammit. Surely someone would see him hurting her and call the police.

"See that big bastard coming this way? He works for the man you let use your body. He's had men following you all week. Did you know that? When he gets here, you need to tell him that you're fine, that this is just a little lovers' spat, and you don't need his help."

Like hell she would. At this point, she'd take anyone in this marketplace over her stupid ex. Her gaze stayed riveted to the man coming toward her. As he got closer, she recognised him as the guy who'd driven the car when Daniil took her home after their night together. What was his name? Viktor something?

"I suggest you take your hands off Julietta. Mr. Mikhailov will not be happy to hear you've hurt her."

Holy shit. Daniil's last name was Mikhailov? As in the Mikhailov Corporation that owned more real estate and businesses in and around Sydney than she could count? Everyone in Sydney knew that name. Hell, you'd have to have been living under a rock for the past ten years to not have.

"Juli is my fiancée, and we're just having a little lovers' spat. Isn't that right, babe?"

He'd lowered her arm so she wasn't forced to stand on her tiptoes, but he'd tightened his grip on her wrist to the point she wondered if he was going to break it. She gave Viktor a pleading look as she shook her head slightly.

"Please."

She hoped Rodger thought she was agreeing with him while she prayed Viktor could see she wasn't okay with this situation at all and would interfere. Hell, if Daniil's man could get her away from Rodger safely, she'd agree to go on as many dates as the man wanted. He would have more than earned it.

After Julietta refused his dinner invitation for last night, Daniil had planned to surprise her as she finished up at the markets today. He was determined to take her out on a date, and he'd hoped that if he caught her in person, she wouldn't be able to turn him down to his face.

That plan changed when he received a text from Viktor letting him know her bastard of an ex had approached her at her stall. He'd been at home, preparing things for her arrival later, but dropped it all to rush to the markets. Since their night together, he'd finally done a little digging into her past. She'd grown up tough even before her mother committed suicide when she'd been only eighteen. Rodger was one of only two serious boyfriends she'd ever had. He'd also confirmed that she'd walked out on her ex after he'd hit her. She was a strong woman, but he wasn't sure if Rodger had something that would make her go back to him. No way would Daniil lose his girl to a womanising piece of shit who liked to use his fists on those weaker than himself.

Both Viktor and his cousin, Yury, worked for Daniil and lived in the guest house on his property. Yury was home, so Daniil grabbed him on his way out. He wanted to put a little show on to warn Rodger to not mess with his girl ever again. It was unfortunate that the place was too populated to take care of the issue in the way he'd really like to, but they'd make it work.

Within minutes, they were parked and rushing toward where he knew Julietta had her stall. They came up behind Rodger, who held his Julietta in what looked like a painful grip if the tense set of her shoulders was any indication. Viktor spotted them, and with a quick hand signal, told him he needed to move in fast.

"I'll handle this myself."

Normally, he would be fine to allow Yury to take care of any troublemakers of Rodger's level, but he wanted this bastard to know he was not a man afraid of getting his hands dirty to protect what, or who, was his.

Daniil stalked up behind Rodger, and before the other man realised he was in trouble, Daniil reached up and wrapped his palm over the top of his shoulder, digging his fingers in hard above the man's collarbone. With a curse, Rodger released Julietta and his shoulder slumped down with the pain Daniil was inflicting with his hold. Viktor quickly pulled her away from Rodger, gently guiding her over to the seat she had at the rear of her small stall. Daniil knew his friend would be assessing any injuries she might have.

"Consider this your only warning, Mr.

Dirk. Touch what is mine again, and it will not end well for you. Do we understand each other?"

The little bastard tried to twist out of his hold, but Daniil kept his grip firm. This wasn't Daniil's first time doing something like this, as Rodger should well know. He gave the man a shake when he stayed silent.

"Juli is not yours. She's mine. My fiancée!"

Daniil leaned down so his lips were close to Rodger's ear. "You raised your fist to her, so that erased any claim you may have had. She no longer wears your ring, no longer wishes to have anything to do with you. Show some dignity and leave her alone. She will not be funding any of your endeavours ever again."

Daniil wasn't sure if Rodger realised he controlled most of the illegal gambling in this part of Sydney. The bastard *should* know with how much he gambled, but if he didn't, he was about to find out because after this little stunt, along with his earlier attack on Julietta, Daniil would be making some phone calls. The reason his Julietta was currently stuck living in a share house with three other women was because this piece of shit had spent all her money placing bets on things he clearly knew nothing about.

Using his grip on his shoulder, Daniil turned him to face Yury.

"Yury, please make sure Mr. Dirk gets home safely."

The grin on his friend's face was not pleasant. Daniil quietly chuckled at the shudder that ran through Rodger's body as he handed him over to Yury.

"Yes, sir. I'll escort him to his home and make sure he's settled in."

With a nod, Daniil dismissed them and turned to focus on his girl. Viktor was still checking her wrist, which looked red and a little swollen. With three long strides, Daniil was at her side.

"Julietta, *solnyshka moto*, I swear trouble follows you."

He leaned in to press a kiss to her temple, loving how she tilted her head up to give him better access. He stroked his knuckles down her cheek.

"Viktor, does she need a doctor?"

His friend shook his head. "I don't believe so. Some ice would help reduce the swelling, but I don't believe he broke her wrist."

Daniil nodded before he pressed a finger gently under her chin to tilt her face up. She looked so fragile in that moment, and he wanted nothing more than to whisk her away, take her to his home where he could keep her locked away and safe from the evils of the world.

"Are you all right, *solnyshka moto*?"

She licked her lips, drawing his attention to them. "Yeah. Thanks to Viktor." She paused a moment, looking into his eyes. "About that—what was he doing here?"

He looked deep into her gaze and knew he couldn't lie his way out of this. She'd already worked it out.

"How about you join me for dinner tonight, and I'll explain to you why you now have a bodyguard?"

She looked torn for a moment. He knew she was trying hard to be all I'm-an-island, but he also knew she was naturally curious and would want to know why he'd put a guard on her. She was also feisty enough she would want to rip into him about taking control of her life without her permission. He hoped being in a public restaurant would limit her reaction on that front.

He wasn't sure how he would get her to see how precious she was to him already, but he needed to work it out quickly. He wasn't sure beginning the conversation by explaining how he had enemies who would harm her was going to help his cause, but it couldn't be helped.

"C'mon, Julietta, these markets are no place for airing private matters, and we've made quite a spectacle as it is. Join me for dinner. I promise I will explain everything."

She tensed on a gasp before her gaze scanned the area around them. He didn't need to look. He knew a number of people were watching them.

"Okay. One dinner, and you explain why you seem to think you now own me. Oh, and I need your phone number."

Grinning, he leaned down again, this time pressing a kiss to her lips. "You say that like it's a bad thing, *solnyshka moto*. Would being mine really be so bad?"

"I will not ever be owned. I'm a person, Daniil, not a pet. And what do you keep calling me?"

"*Solnyshka moto?*"

"Yeah, that."

"It's another Russian endearment. I called you 'my sun'." He gave one of her brightly coloured braids a gentle tug. "I'll come back and help you pack up at closing, and then we'll go out for dinner. Viktor will remain with you until then."

She pulled out her phone. "I still want your number."

He smirked at her but rattled off his digits. "Send me a text so I have yours."

As she did that, Daniil stood tall and glanced around for his friend. He spotted him strolling toward them with something in his hands. He frowned as he tried to see what it was, then smiled when he worked it out.

"Here's an ice pack for your wrist." Viktor handed her the Ziplock bag of ice he'd managed to find.

He gave his man a nod. "Thank you, Viktor. I need to go take care of some things but will be back before closing. I'll see you both then."

After he gave his girl one last kiss, he turned and left. Not only did he need to finish his preparations for tonight, he also now needed to make some calls to make sure Rodger was going to find it difficult to feed his gambling addiction anywhere near Sydney. It was a pity the man had forced the public confrontation today, or Daniil would have simply made him disappear. But now he would need to avoid him for a while before he could take care of the bastard in a permanent manner.

CHAPTER SEVEN

Juli couldn't believe where Daniil had brought her for dinner, although in hindsight she should have expected something this fancy. She'd never been to the exclusive Italian restaurant, Flamma Oceano, which sat on the coast at the southern end of Bondi Beach. Since she could see it from the surf where she spent so much of her time, she'd certainly checked it out plenty, but she'd never even considered that she might be able to afford to dine here. And not only had Daniil managed to get them a table at the last minute, but they were also out on the deck in a secluded corner that afforded them some privacy.

"How did you get a table here on such short notice?"

A horrible thought had the blood draining from her face. She hoped he hadn't hurt someone in order to obtain it. After him scaring off her attackers in some mysterious manner and the casual violence he'd used against Rodger, she wasn't sure what to think about how he got jobs done. It was why she'd left his phone number with Jess. If she didn't return home, her friend would have a starting point to track her down.

He gave her a smirk. "Nothing as nefarious as you're thinking, I'm sure. I went to school with the owner. Nico and I are friends, so I simply called and asked for a favour. He delivered."

She was fairly certain they weren't merely friends. From what she'd seen so far, Daniil didn't seem like the type to have innocent friendships. A waiter came and delivered entrées they hadn't ordered. Juli raised an eyebrow in question.

"When I booked, I placed our order. If you don't like what I've selected, I can get something else prepared for you. I don't like to be bothered with waiters while I'm trying to enjoy my night, so prefer to pre-order my meal when I can. This is their Filetto di Pesce. The fish is Murray Cod."

She nodded because really, what could she say to that? How rich was this guy? Was he really *the* Mr. Mikhailov?

"So, your last name is really Mikhailov?"

He gave her another smirk. "Yes, Julietta, I am really the Mr. Mikhailov behind Mikhailov Corp. I gather you've heard of me, or at least my company?"

That made her roll her eyes with a chuckle. "Of course, I've heard of you and your company. I just didn't know what you looked like to realise it was you." She shook her head. "I have no idea what you want with me. I'm nobody, with barely a cent to my name, while you ... Hell, you're richer than God!"

He reached across the small table and cupped her cheek in his palm. "A person's wealth does not equal their worth. And you, *solnyshka moto*, are a rare and priceless gem in this world."

He ran his thumb over her lips before releasing her to return to eating his entrée. Meanwhile, it took Juli a full minute to be able to breathe again, then another before she could focus enough to lift her fork and eat. She chewed on auto pilot, barely able to register what she was eating with the way her mind spun. He was treating her like a princess, while he was clearly ruthless with everyone else in his world. What would he be like when he got angry with her? Would he get violent? She'd overheard what he'd said to Rodger... that by raising his fist to her he'd lost any right to her. Did that mean he himself wasn't violent toward women?

"I can see you have questions, *krasivaya*. Ask me anything."

She swallowed the last bite of her fish and lowered her fork. *Where to start?*

"I have so many, I'm not sure where to begin." She paused for a moment to wipe her mouth with her napkin. "Why did you give me a bodyguard? I thought you handled those two thugs last week. You told me not to worry about them."

He set his own cutlery down, and within seconds a waitress appeared and cleared the table. *Wow. Now that was fast service.*

"It is true that you won't ever have to worry about those particular thugs again. But since I interfered and saved you, then took you to my home, it's become known that you are important to me. And in my world, there are those who will happily use you to hurt me. So, for your protection, I arranged for you to be guarded. They have been instructed to stay back and not interfere unless you require their aid. Like today."

She rubbed her temples. She was struggling to wrap her head around all he'd just said.

"And to think I was grateful you saved me, but it turns out I'm in more danger now than I was before."

She'd mumbled under her breath, but the way he stiffened in his seat indicated he'd heard her. She winced. *Oops.* Offending him probably wasn't in her best interest.

"You are now safer than you have ever been. Tell me, Julietta, what would have happened today if Viktor wasn't there to stop Rodger?"

Anger rose up. "He only came after me today because he'd seen your men around me all week."

He tilted his head at her, as though she'd

somehow just confirmed his point when she hadn't.

"So he's been watching you for at least the past week. Personally, I suspect he's been doing it for a lot longer. Did you know your ex has quite the gambling problem? At a guess, he's run out of money, so came to you in the hopes you'd give him more. Or perhaps he is truly stupid and wanted to ransom you to me for the funds he needs." He shrugged. "Either way, I won't allow him near you to try again."

She clenched her hands into fists on the table. "What did you do to him? Actually, first, tell me what you did to those men the other night."

He sighed and closed his eyes for a moment. "I don't believe you really want to know, nor do I think you *should* know. But since you keep asking me, I'll tell you. I killed them, then had one of my men help me dispose of the bodies. They were nothing but scum, and the world is better off without them. Your ex is still breathing, for the moment. However, he will now find gambling in Sydney rather difficult no matter how much money he has."

Juli's mouth hung open at his brutal words. He spoke of death with such casualness. A tremor ran through her, and suddenly she wanted to leave. She didn't want to be part of his world if it was filled with such bloodshed.

"I need to go now."

She pushed back her seat, but Daniil was at her side by the time she stood. He'd been expecting her to react badly to what he'd been forced to do in order to save her. With a hand wrapped around the back of her neck, he brought her forward until she was pressed against him. She raised her palms, pushing them against his chest, but no way was he going to let her shove him away from her.

"Don't run from me, *krasivaya*. I will never do you harm. I only hurt those who deserve it, never an innocent. I will not ever get you mixed up in my business, and I will never again tell you when I have had to get my hands dirty. I only told you about those men because you seemed to be obsessing over it, and I refuse to lie to you. I want you in my bed and in my life. I want to explore this chemistry we have between us."

Before she could tell him some other bullshit reason she couldn't be with him, Daniil lowered his mouth to hers and devoured her, loving her taste and the way her scent filled his lungs and made him feel lighter. Nipping at her lower lip, he pulled back from her.

"When I was a young boy, my mama told me that when I met the woman who was meant for me, I'd know. I thought she was crazy at the time, and I didn't understand what she meant until I saw and spoke with you at the markets." He paused to rub his thumb over her kiss-swollen lower lip. "You need to understand, *krasivaya*, a man like me, in my position, does not willingly take on a weakness, yet here I am, doing whatever I can to have you stay with me. And make no mistake, Julietta, you are already my biggest weakness."

A cute little frown wrinkled her brow. "How in the world did you come to that conclusion? We barely know each other. And if you're so worried about being seen as weak because of me, the solution is simple. Let me go."

Daniil growled at her. Didn't she understand? He couldn't do that, and even if he did, it wouldn't matter. Word would have spread by now that he'd shown interest in her. Even if he never touched her again, she would be targeted.

"You don't make me look weak, Julietta, but rather are a weakness, a vulnerability. I have no family that I hold dear. I don't even have a pet. Those who want to get to me have been waiting a long time for me to show them a way to hurt me, and by rescuing you, taking such an interest in you, I've done just that. So, even if I could let you walk away from me, it wouldn't make any difference. You will be a target now."

She stilled, tilting her head to the side as she frowned at him. The action made him nervous enough he loosened his hold on her. What was she thinking now?

"No family? At all?"

He shook his head. "None."

"Neither have I."

She whispered her words before stepping back and sitting in her seat. Daniil followed her lead and returned to his place opposite her. Within moments, a waiter brought out their main course, and they stayed silent until the man left. He wanted to ask how she came to be alone but wasn't sure how to word it so she didn't shut down on him. He knew about her mother's death, but she didn't know he knew. And he couldn't find anything on her father when he'd researched her background.

In the end, he decided he'd just eat his meal and let her decide when to speak. They'd nearly finished when she did finally break the silence.

"Is your family back in Russia?"

He finished his mouthful before responding. "I have relatives back in Russia, but no one I'm close with. My parents immigrated to Australia when I was four years old. Then, when I was twelve, they were in a car accident that killed them both. I have no siblings, so now it's just me."

He hoped she didn't ask for more details about the years after he lost his parents. But as he watched the expressions flit over her face, he knew she would. He took another mouthful of food to postpone the inevitable.

"What about a foster family?"

He took his time chewing, trying to find a way to word things.

"I wasn't in the system long. The family I was placed with wasn't a good fit." Understatement of the year. That family had been horrific. Both parents and the older teenage boy had treated him like a convenient punching bag. He cleared his throat. "I ran away and lived on the streets, doing what I had to in order to survive."

He'd worked his arse off to rise up from nothing to what he had now. He wasn't ashamed of where he'd come from, but he suspected his sweet Julietta wouldn't appreciate the fact he'd sold drugs and gotten his hands very dirty over the years to get where he was. But it was worth it. Every single nasty thing he'd ever done. Because he knew he'd never again go hungry, never again not know where he was going to sleep at night and whether it was safe. It also put him in a position to be able to provide everything required to keep his family safe and cared for, when he had one. He really wanted Julietta to be that family.

He finished the last of his food, and after

putting down his cutlery, looked up to hold her gaze. She had tears in her eyes. He frowned. Were they for him? The fact she was upset over his childhood floored him, and made him desperate to get the focus off him and back onto her.

"Ah, *krasivaya*, don't cry for me. I'm fine. I survived, and it made me who I am. What about you? Did you grow up in the system?"

She shook her head and blinked away the unshed tears.

"I was raised by my mum. I have no idea who my dad is. Mum, she, ah... well, she always had an eye on the door, waiting for something better to come along. Kind of ironic really, that the first time a man shoved her aside for someone else, she reacted by taking her own life."

Shock had him swallowing his mouthful of wine wrong, and he started coughing. She spoke about her mother's suicide and the reason behind it as though it were no big deal. Once he got his breath back, he looked up to find her calmly eating the last of her dessert with her gaze locked on her plate.

"Julietta? Look at me, please. Did I hear

you right? Your mother took her own life? How old were you?"

He needed her to tell him all the details, so then he wouldn't have to worry about slipping up and admitting to knowing things she hadn't told him. With slow, steady moves that showed him she was not calm at all, Julietta set her fork down and wiped her mouth with her napkin.

"You heard me right. Mum's last boyfriend dumped her for a younger model. She took it really hard, and I found her in the tub. She'd downed an entire bottle of sleeping pills. She was pronounced dead on arrival at the hospital. I was eighteen."

He knew from her licence that she was currently thirty-two, so she'd been without family for fourteen years. He shook his head, not wanting to end their night on negative thoughts.

"I'm sorry for your loss, *krasivaya*, and I must say, I'm impressed at how you've kept your positive outlook after all you've been through."

That was the truth. He certainly didn't see the world as she did. Even after everything, she appeared to only see the good around her. Until meeting her, Daniil hadn't believed there was much good left in the world for a very long damn time. He'd seen and done too much evil to have ever had that particular illusion in his life.

As he ran his gaze over her, from her purple-blue hair, her sexy little pink dress, to her neon-blue nails, he had the thought that she was the light to his dark. That if he could work out a way to keep her, she might just be able to breathe some life back into his cold heart.

CHAPTER EIGHT

"Come spend the night with me, *krasivaya*."

Juli struggled to get her brain to function enough to respond. Daniil had her pressed up against the rear door of his sleek, black town car and had just given her another of his soul-stealing kisses. She both loved and hated those kisses. They stole her ability to think and melted her insides until she forgot why she didn't want a man in her life.

She shook her head in an attempt to clear it as he moved to nibble along her jaw, up to her ear.

"You have nothing to fear with me, Julietta." He moved one of his thighs between hers, rubbing against her aching centre, which made her groan. "Follow your body, *krasivaya*. Let me take care of you. Give you what you need."

Should she give in? She knew precisely how well he'd take care of her sexually, although she'd probably struggle to teach her surfing lessons tomorrow if she did. That thought was fortunately enough to cool her body sufficiently so she could form words.

"I can't. I have to work in the morning, and if I go home with you, I'll get no sleep and be barely able to walk by morning, let alone able to teach other people how to stand on a surfboard."

He growled low, the deep sound vibrating through her entire being. She loved that sound almost as much as his kisses. It would be so easy to lean on this man, to cede control and allow him to take care of her. Images of her mother flashed through her mind, of how she was always on the hunt for someone who could take care of her, give her everything she thought she needed or wanted. Of how she put more effort into making sure she looked perfect for those men than she did into parenting or caring for her only daughter.

"You will be back in my bed where you

belong soon, *solnyshka moto*. But for tonight, I'll let you go rest. We will talk tomorrow."

With that, he stepped back, took her hand in his and walked her to her door. He was full of contradictions, one minute doing everything he could to seduce her out of her knickers, and the next, he was this perfect gentleman who walked her to her door before kissing her goodnight.

With her thoughts in turmoil, she closed the door and leaned back against it once she was inside. What the bloody hell was she meant to do with this man?

"You okay, Juli? Have to be honest, I wasn't actually expecting you back tonight."

She banged her head back against the door twice before she turned to face Jess.

"I'm so fucked."

Jess smirked at her. "Well, that was why I figured you wouldn't be back until the morning ... I'm guessing the issue is really the fact that you're currently not getting fucked, yeah?"

That had her barking out a laugh before she moved to drop down onto the couch beside her friend.

"Something like that. Daniil has me in

knots. I don't know what to do with him. I swore after all that shit with Rodger, I'd steer clear of men." And because of her mother, but she didn't want to get into that with Jess. "Especially older, powerful, strong ones like Daniil."

Jess sighed. "But he is sex on a stick, babe. Not sure I could say no to that if he came calling for me. If you don't want to even try to see if it works long-term with him, why don't you just fuck him out of your system? Enjoy the moment, babe. Because I bet that man rocks in bed."

Juli nodded before rising up off the couch. "That he does. Rocks in the shower, too." She gave Jess a smirk and wink. "I'm going to bed. Gotta work in the morning. Night."

Jess mumbled something under her breath, but Juli didn't hear it as she wandered back toward the bathroom where she quickly washed her face and brushed her teeth before she headed for her room and locked herself in. Share houses sucked. She trusted Jess, of course, but the two backpackers, not so much. It didn't help they seemed to switch out every few weeks so she never really got to know them.

Tossing her bag in the corner, she put her phone on her bedside table before pulling off her dress and dumping it in her laundry bin. Her bra followed, and then she slipped into bed and stared at the ceiling, unable to sleep. Thoughts of Daniil kept her mind too busy to relax.

When her phone beeped with a message, she grabbed it from the table to see who was messaging her.

> Changed my mind. Need u here. Coming 2 get u.

Growling, she rolled her eyes. He was so fucking demanding! Although, it *was* nice to know she wasn't the only one caught up in knots.

> I'm not going anywhere. I'm already in bed. Talk to you later.

She held her breath waiting for his response. Maybe she shouldn't have said she was in bed.

> What r u wearing?

That made her laugh. Such a typical guy thing to say. She took a couple deep breaths as she thought about how she should respond. She was only wearing a cute little pair of knickers, but should she be honest or have some fun with him? He got her so worked up every time she saw him that it seemed only fair he got a turn at being riled up. *Right?*

> Nothing but a lacy blue g-string. U?

A moment later her phone rang and chuckling, she answered.

"Hello?"

"You serious or just messing with me?"

With a grin, she wriggled down further in her bed. "Bit of both. I'm wearing blue knickers, not a G-string, and the only reason I still have them on is pure laziness. Why? Did my message get you all worked up?"

"Yes. Imagining you in nothing but a scrap of lace gets me hard, Julietta. Want to put your fingers to work and let me know if you're wet for me?"

Arousal zipped down her spine. Listening to Daniil's sexy accent talking dirty to her definitely got her motor running. Without further thought, she ran her fingers down her torso, slipping beneath the lace and over her clit. She arched her back on a groan. Damn, she was horny.

"Like the sound of that groan, *krasivaya*. You wet? Or you need a little more dirty talk to get you going?"

"So wet."

"Yeah, fuck. You look so hot touching yourself. Could watch you all fucking day."

She slipped her fingers lower, teasing her opening with two fingers.

"How'd you know what I look like?"

"Because I fucking watch you do it every damn night. You did it after we had sex. I came out of the bathroom to find you spread out on my bed working yourself over. Sexiest thing I've seen in a long time."

She froze at his words and, pulling her hand free, she sat up, frowning. "What do you mean, you watch me every night? You haven't fucking bugged my room or something crazy, have you?"

Oh, if he was spying on her she'd kill him. No idea how she'd manage it, but she'd find a way.

"Ah fuck. I didn't mean to say that. *Yebat-kopat*!"

She was pretty sure that Russian word wasn't an endearment. Was he really swearing at her in two languages?

"No idea what you just said, but it's not making me feel any better here, Daniil. What have you done?"

"I just cursed in Russian." He sighed. "You looked so fucking hot, I grabbed my phone and took a little video—"

Fury exploded through her, and her mouth started moving before her brain re-engaged.

"You fucking arsehole! You fucking videoed me? So help me if you've uploaded that to a fucking porn site or something, I swear I will cut your balls off!"

"*Solnyshka moto*, I promise, no one has seen it but me. No one ever will—"

With a voice like ice, she cut him off again. "Don't you dare ever call me any of your bullshit Russian endearments. In fact, you know what? Don't ever call me again. And delete that damn video. I can't believe you would do that! Fuck."

She hung up the phone, not caring he

was still trying to talk to her. When her phone rang a second later, she screamed and threw it across the room. It landed in her laundry bin, and she hoped it didn't break, but she'd worry about that later. *Fucking men!* They were all pigs. Slipping on a pair of yoga pants and a baggy T-shirt, she left her room in search of alcohol.

She was way too angry to sleep now anyway.

♛

Daniil let loose a string of curses. He was so furious, it ended up being a mix of Russian and English. Viktor cleared his throat.

"You need some help, D? Because if you keep this shit up, you're gonna scare away all your staff."

He bared his teeth at his friend on a growl. He didn't give a fuck. It had been over twelve hours since he'd screwed up with Julietta, and she was still declining all his calls. Yury was on guard duty, and he'd reported that she'd refused to talk to him or listen to anything he'd tried to say. Why had he said anything about that damn video? At least he didn't mention the photos he'd taken... He rubbed a palm over the back of his neck. Why he'd taken the damn video in the first place was a better question. He knew women didn't like that shit. *Dammit.*

"That, right there. That's why the girls called me. You need to cut the shit. Personally, I think it's funny as hell, but if you want to keep this part of your company running, I'd suggest dialling it back, yeah?"

He blew out a breath. He knew Viktor was right. He was working from his real estate office today, and he did need this business to function at a profitable level. Not something that would happen if he scared off all his staff.

"Fine. Come in and shut the door."

Once they were enclosed in his office, Daniil went and pulled out the vodka. After pouring out two glasses, he returned to his desk, handing off one drink to Viktor before sitting down and taking a large mouthful. He focused on the burn as the alcohol flowed down his throat.

"I fucked up with Julietta. Now she won't answer my calls. Won't talk to Yury either."

Viktor calmly sipped his drink like all

was well in the world, which made him angry all over again. Because it wasn't, at least not in *his* world. He felt like he was at the edge of his control, ready to snap at any moment.

"What exactly did you do to her?"

After downing the rest of his vodka in one shot, he told his friend about the video, about her finding out. His response was to raise an eyebrow and smirk. He knew what Viktor was silently asking.

"No, you can't see it. No one is seeing it. *Ever.*"

He had it encrypted so deeply no one would ever be able to gain access, other than him. And if he did manage to get her back, he'd delete it along with the photos she didn't know about. He was only keeping them for now because he had a horrible feeling they might be the only things he would have left to remember her by soon.

"She said not to *call* her. Stop being a coward and go get her. She's always wandering off someplace alone to take photos. Get Yury—or whoever happens to be on guard duty—to tell you next time she does, and go get her while she's alone and make it up to her. I have to admit, she might still tell you to fuck off. Taking a video like that without the girl's consent is fucking asking for trouble. Even you should know better than to pull a stunt like that."

Daniil shrugged. He was used to ruling his world and doing what he wanted when he wanted. Before Julietta, he hadn't cared what a woman thought. Nor had he ever wanted to video one so he could watch it later, on repeat. He growled. Julietta was screwing with his head in a big way.

"You really like this girl, huh? You thinking of settling down? Having a family with her? Assuming you can get her to forgive your stupid arse."

He paused and looked over at Viktor. "Yeah, I think I am. Julietta's special. She makes me feel different. Better." He scrubbed his palms over his face. "I know I shouldn't take her. She'll always be a target. A weakness others will try to use against me and the company."

Viktor shrugged. "We'll handle any threats. This life? It's lonely as fuck, and I can see the appeal of settling down. Coming home to a house with warmth and life in it, a wife waiting for your return? That sounds like a slice of heaven to me. Money's nice and all, but it won't keep you warm at night."

He scoffed. "Well, it does when you use it to pay the power bill."

Viktor rolled his eyes. "You know what I mean."

"Yeah, I know. You sound like you've been thinking about it too. You got a girl stashed away somewhere?"

Viktor stood and stretched out his neck. "Nah, I'm single like I've always been. You and your girl just got me thinking, that's all. I'm going to head out. But you need to try to stop scaring the natives, yeah?"

Daniil shook his head. "Fine, I'll rein it in. Thanks, man."

With a nod, Viktor was gone, and once more Daniil found himself alone. He'd never minded before. In fact, he'd always preferred his own company. But since meeting his Julietta, he often found himself wishing she were with him. He thought over what Viktor had said, and he had to agree, coming home to a loving wife welcoming him would be a nice thing to have.

He'd really fucked up with Julietta, and

he couldn't just go grab her off the street. She'd go crazy on him. No, he needed to ease the way a little. She'd liked the flowers he'd sent her. He'd send some more today, then maybe some jewellery or perfume tomorrow. See if he could soften her up a little over the course of the work week, and then on Saturday, when she was out searching for the perfect photo, he'd go to her. Force her to listen to him.

Even if he had to spend the entire weekend grovelling, he would win back his lady.

CHAPTER NINE

It had been a long week, but finally it was Saturday, and Juli was free to drive up the coast to take some photos. Since leaving Rodger, she actually got to drive her little red Suzuki Vitara a lot more often. It was getting old but still ran well. She experienced the most wonderful sense of freedom when the roof was off, and the wind blew through her hair. No matter how crappy she felt, going for a drive always improved her mood. Even when there was a noisy as hell big, black Harley following her.

She cranked up her stereo in an attempt to block out the sound of the bike roaring behind her. Despite the fact she'd refused all contact with Daniil, he still insisted on her having a bodyguard each day. It was beginning to drive her nuts. Every morning, she'd tell whichever bloke he'd sent that he didn't need to stay. She was certain they had better things to do with their day. But without fail, they would simply shake their heads and stick to her like glue. Yury had tried to plead Daniil's case for him that first morning after their disastrous phone call, but she didn't want to hear it. She was done with that man. Just thinking about the fact he'd videoed her masturbating so he could watch it again and again made her blood boil. How dare he! She wasn't some bloody porn star.

Wasn't her fault the damn man made her ache just thinking about him. Even now, after what he'd done, her body lit up like a firecracker whenever she thought about him. Which was often, especially now she had a room full of flowers and various other gifts. He'd been sending her stuff every day all week, each item arriving with a simple note saying he was sorry and asking for forgiveness. She wanted to stay mad at him, to hold on to her fury like a security blanket, but he was beginning to get to her with all the little gifts he'd sent, and the fact he still wanted her protected.

Sighing, she pulled off the road onto a little dirt track she knew ran to a small parking area. From there it was only a short walk to a section of clifftop that would give her excellent views of the ocean. She'd caught some great photos of dolphins here before. As she rolled to a stop, she idly wondered if Viktor would be pissed at having to take his bike on a dirt road. Then she shrugged off the thought. It wasn't like she'd made him follow her out here. She grabbed her camera bag and hopped out of her car, pocketing the keys. Seeing that Viktor was on his phone, she didn't say anything to him before she headed toward the clifftop. When she got there, she stood with her eyes closed for a minute, just taking the fresh, salty air deep within her lungs. She allowed the tension of the week to ease from her muscles before she opened her eyes, and looked around.

"Oh, awesome!"

A kilometre or so up the coast there was a section of rock that jutted out from the cliff into the ocean, and since she'd been here last, some of it had eroded away. Now, there was a beautiful archway. Dropping down to her knees, she quickly got her camera out and fitted the right lens to catch her find. When she looked back up, she got an idea for a great shot. Lying down on her stomach, she moved over to the edge of the cliff to line up the shot. At this angle, she could see breaking waves through the archway. She made a mental note to come back at dawn one day soon, to get this shot with the sunrise colours reflecting off the water. The result would be outstanding.

She was so engrossed in getting the perfect angle, she didn't hear anything warn her before a large hand roughly grabbed her ankle and ripped her backward. A cry left her as her bare belly scraped over rocks and she lost her grip on her camera for a moment. Seeing her most prized possession land heavily on the rough ground before she could snatch it back up into her grip, had her fury spiking.

"What the fuck?"

As she cursed, she kicked out with her free leg, happy when her foot made contact hard enough to dislodge their grip.

Scrambling to her feet, she turned to face her attacker, her heart jumping when she saw who it was. She'd been hoping it was just Viktor, who'd maybe panicked at seeing her so close to the cliff.

But it wasn't Viktor. Far from it.

"What the fuck are you doing here, Rodger?"

He rubbed his forearm where she'd kicked him, as he smirked at her.

"I'm here to collect what's mine."

She rolled her eyes. "Considering I haven't been yours in months, it can't be me, so whatever it is, take it and piss off."

She ran her gaze around the area. Where was Viktor? While she hadn't known the man long, it had been long enough that she knew he didn't take his bodyguard duties lightly. He should be here.

"You're mine until *I* say otherwise."

Her breath caught as she refocused on her ex. Had he lost his mind? His left eye had a twitch to it that he couldn't seem to control. His hair was slicked back as per usual, but his skin looked paler, kind of like he was strung out on something.

Great. That's all I need.

"That's bullshit, and you know it. I left you, moved out." She kept her voice low and calm, as she tried to work out what game he was playing. "What did you do to Viktor?"

An evil smile formed on his face, but before he said a word, strong arms came around her torso from behind. She found herself pinned back against a solid chest.

"Viktor won't be much use to anyone anymore. Can't wait to see Daniil's face when he finds out I've taken out his oh, so precious right-hand man and snatched his woman."

Juli sucked in a breath as the man behind her spoke. He'd killed Viktor? How? That man was so big and strong and careful. He was always on the alert for threats. Rodger stepping in close, bringing her focus back to him and her situation.

"You have no clue who you're fucking, do you, babe?"

She glared at her ex but stayed silent.

"I mean, sure, everyone knows about the real estate shit. But I bet you have no fucking idea about his other income avenues ... the drugs and gambling he controls, the killings and beatings he does for money. Fuck, babe, he's probably got big plans for you on your back once he gets you hooked on him!"

The guy holding her chuckled, lifting his arms so they pushed her breasts up in her bikini to the point they were nearly popping out for the world to see. "Can't blame him there. It's what I'd do with a hot little piece of arse like you. Rodger, take this fucking bikini off. I wanna see what we're gonna play with later."

A shudder ran through her as her ex slipped his hands inside her bikini and palmed both her breasts. He squeezed them roughly enough to bring tears to her eyes before he lifted them out of their coverings. He gave each of her nipples a pinch before he stepped back, chuckling.

"Let's get outta here, so we can start the fun. Can't wait to show that prick a video of us using her."

What the fuck was with men wanting to video her lately? Bile rose up her throat as she thought about what these two bastards were planning to do to her. She needed to get free and run. It was her only hope. When the one holding her moved his head back from looking over her shoulder at her boobs, she tilted her face down, hoping they would think she was accepting defeat. Then she threw her head back as fast and hard as she could. Pain flared as she made contact, but the grunt and curse of the man made it worth it, especially when his grip loosened for a moment, enabling her to pull free. But Rodger was right there in front of her. As he went to grab her, she brought up the hand that held her camera, grateful she'd kept hold of it, and, wincing over the damage she was about to inflict on it, smashed it into the side of his head.

"Fucking hell, Juli!"

He stumbled back, and she took advantage and bolted away from them. Unfortunately, she didn't get far. Two steps later, she jerked to a stop as someone took a solid grip of a fistful of hair that she'd left down today. They pulled her head back until she whimpered at the pain in her neck and skull.

"Fucking little bitch."

It was the man who'd grabbed her before, but his voice was different now, like he was having to breathe through his mouth. She hoped she'd broken the bastard's nose.

Rodger came at her front again, shaking his head and cursing. He didn't give her any warning, just walked straight up to her and punched her hard in the stomach. All the breath rushed from her lungs as pain rocketed through her. She wanted to curl up in a ball on the ground, but the bastard holding on to her hair prevented any movement. Tears welled and trickled down her cheeks. She was in so much trouble. And this time, Daniil wasn't here to come to the rescue.

As though she'd thought him into being, a moment later she was sure she heard Daniil growling, but she ignored it, assuming it was just her mind playing a trick and imagining it. Then a loud crack split the air and Rodger flew sideways and away from her. With a curse, her captor threw her to the side where she landed heavily on the ground. Her elbow struck a rock, and more pain flared.

Everything hurt, and on instinct, she curled up into a ball and squeezed her eyes shut. Maybe this was all just a bad dream, and she'd wake up back in her room soon.

Yeah. Waking up anytime now would be great.

Rage like he'd never known coursed through Daniil as he came upon the scene. Viktor had rung to tell him the location when Julietta had stopped to take photos so he could come and surprise her, but after that he'd been silent, not responding to any of his messages or calls. That was highly unusual, so Daniil had gotten himself armed up and come running. Now he was here, he was glad he'd stopped to grab Yury on his way.

Soon after pulling up, they found Viktor unconscious with a bullet wound in his shoulder, and it looked like he'd been hit over the side of the head with something heavy. The gunshot wound was a little high to have hit his heart, but the man had lost a lot of blood and didn't look good. Daniil lowered down to check for a pulse, relieved to find one. It was faint, but there.

"Yury, I need you to get Viktor loaded into the van. Then come find me. We'll get

Julietta, then get out of here. We'll call the doc once we're on our way."

Nodding, Yury went to his cousin as Daniil headed toward a path that led through a thin line of bush. The coastline must be right on the other side, and at this height, he guessed it was a cliff rather than a beach that he'd find himself on. As he moved, he checked his gun and flicked off the safety. No need for a silencer out here, thank fuck. When he broke through the bush to the clearing on the cliff edge, a growl rumbled up his throat.

Julietta's top had been pulled down to reveal her breasts, and he'd arrived just in time to see her ex, Rodger, land a hard punch to her stomach, while another bastard he knew all too well was holding her by her hair. Tony had Julietta's head arched back, far enough it had to be hurting her neck. They hadn't seen or heard him yet, so he made the most of that fact and lined up a shot. Julietta was too close to Tony, so he couldn't shoot that arsehole without risking hurting his girl. Taking a moment, he lined up the side of Rodger's torso. He'd have loved to have put a bullet in his skull, but the reality was he was too far away to risk aiming at that small a target. Nope, a torso shot would get him away from her, stop him hurting her.

Daniil's hands were rock-steady as, half a second before he pulled the trigger, Rodger turned toward him, opening up a bigger target. It also meant Rodger saw him, but it was too late. Daniil fired, then was on the move, running over to finish off dealing with the situation. The bullet took Rodger in the upper chest, sending him crashing to the ground, away from Julietta.

Tony saw him coming and roughly threw Julietta to the ground before he reached under his arm, no doubt for his own gun. *Fuck that.* Daniil didn't care why these two had teamed up to take his girl, he just wanted her safe. Lifting his gun, he quickly lined up his shot. He wanted his bullet to land right between Tony's eyes. Daniil was about to squeeze the trigger when he saw Yury come up on the other side of Tony. He held his gun steady, but waited to see what his friend was up to.

"You cocksucking arsehole."

At the sound of Yury's voice, Tony stopped trying to get his gun free of its holster and spun with his fists raised. Stupid bastard didn't even get to throw a single punch before Yury slammed his fist into his already fucked up nose, and he dropped like the sack of shit he was, out cold. Stowing his gun, Daniil rushed over to Julietta, knowing Yury would be watching his back, leaving him to focus solely on his girl. She was barely conscious. As he carefully lifted her from the ground, he pressed a kiss to her temple.

"I've got you, *krasivaya*. You're safe now."

She shuddered for a moment before she relaxed against him, trusting him.

If she wasn't currently injured, he would have been overjoyed. He glanced over at Yury and grinned as he watched him deliver a hard punch to Rodger's face, knocking out the whimpering arsehole.

"Let me get Julietta settled, then I'll come help you load these two. We need to do this shit fast. Viktor needs a doctor sooner rather than later."

"I've bandaged the wound, tried to slow

the blood loss, but yeah, we don't have much time."

He moved as fast as he could back to their SUV and settled Julietta in the front seat.

"*Krasivaya*, I need to leave you for a few minutes, okay? Stay right here, and I'll be back before you know it."

She didn't open her eyes as she curled up into a ball against the seat. He wasn't sure if she was conscious enough to hear him, but Viktor didn't have time to muck around. He sprinted back to the clearing and eyed off the two men, then the cliff. Maybe they could toss the pair of them over the edge?

"Not a good idea, boss. You put a bullet in Rodger. Forensics can identify that shit. And they are both alive, so we need to find out what they were planning to do."

"They're nothing but scum. Doubt anyone will miss either of them, but you're right. Let's load them up and get them locked down before they wake. I don't want to have to deal with either one of them until after I'm sure both Julietta and Viktor will be fine."

He didn't say it, didn't need to. Yury knew as well as he did that neither of those men would ever see the light of day again. They were dead men walking for touching what was his.

CHAPTER TEN

Juli couldn't break through the fog in her mind. Her body was numb while her mind was curiously blank. She was vaguely aware of being lifted, then surrounded by warmth and a scent that wormed past the fog and had her relaxing as the sounds of a car starting filled her ears.

The next time her mind floated to the surface, she was standing in a dimly lit room. Her eyes wouldn't focus, and by the tugs at her body she guessed someone was stripping her. Each breath she took in brought more of that calming scent with it, and she sighed.

"C'mon, *krasivaya*, we need to get you cleaned up, and then the doc will check you over."

She frowned. She knew that voice. Who

was it? Why couldn't she remember? Large, warm hands ran over her body, and then she was being lifted. Her skin came up against a naked chest, and she pressed her palm over one of his pecs. The thudding of his heart reverberated through her palm, and after sighing again, she dropped her head against his shoulder, letting the fog in her mind thicken as it wanted to. She was vaguely aware when it started raining warm, soft rain before the fog completely stole her thoughts.

♛

With a groan, Juli slowly woke, with what had to be the worst hangover she'd ever had. Why had she gotten so drunk? She frowned. She didn't actually recall drinking anything at all. Fingers stroked through her hair, pulling it away from her face.

"*Solnyshka moto*, you ready to wake up for me yet?"

Daniil? What was he doing here? She rolled over, and pain lit up her stomach and head enough to have bile rising up her throat. She gagged, and a moment later, she was dragged to the edge of the bed, and he held her head gently, keeping her hair out of the way as she threw up into a rubbish bin he'd obviously left close by for just this purpose. While her stomach emptied out, memories flashed through her mind. Rodger and that other man... what they'd done to her. When she was through, her body went limp, and Daniil moved her back onto the mattress before he left her. He returned a moment later and wiped her face with a cold washcloth. It felt so good, she groaned in bliss.

She blinked her eyes open to watch as he moved around the room, taking the bin into the bathroom and returning with it freshly rinsed out. He was beautiful and so sweet. She frowned at that thought because he wasn't always sweet. Nope. This was the man who'd taken a video of her without her knowledge. And she hadn't forgotten what Rodger had told her. Considering how easily he handled her attackers the other week, and now Rodger and his mate, she suspected her ex hadn't been lying. How was she meant to process any of this? Especially when her brain was still more than a touch foggy.

He climbed on the bed next to her before reaching over her to the bedside table. He came back with two pills, which he put in her palm before grabbing a glass of water.

"Here, Julietta, take these. They'll help take away some of the pain."

"Why..." She struggled to find words for what she wanted to ask. She wanted to know why he'd taken that video. Had Rodger told the truth? Was he planning to prostitute her out? Why had he been there at the cliff in the first place? Why was she now in his bed? And what had he done to save her this time? Also, was Viktor really dead?

He nudged her hand. He stayed silent, just looking at the pills, until with a sigh, she took them. Probably should have asked what they were, but the fog still floating around her mind had her thoughts tripping all over the place. And honestly, the longer she was awake, the more her body hurt, so as long as the meds took her pain away, she was good with it.

Daniil took the glass and set it back on the table before he helped her to lie back down. She kept her gaze on his face, trying to find answers to all the questions she had floating around her head.

"I had a doctor come and check you over yesterday. Nothing is broken, but you're going to be sore for a while. He gave you something to help you sleep, which you've done for the past" —he looked at his watch — "fourteen hours. Doc said that was normal, that your body and mind needed time to rest and heal."

"Why didn't you take me to the hospital if my injuries are that severe?"

"You got banged up, but nothing serious enough to need hospitalisation. And I have a few of my men already at the hospital keeping Viktor safe. I don't have enough men I fully trust to have you both guarded in such a public place as a hospital, even a private one. You're safer here."

A wave of relief that Viktor wasn't dead had her eyes stinging. Daniil's world was crazy and violent, and she really wanted out of it before it was too late.

"I want to go home."

He cupped her jaw in his palm, rubbing his thumb over her lower lip. "I'm sorry, *krasivaya*, but I can't allow that. It's not safe for you there right now."

"What about Jess? And the others?"

He gave her a small smile. "They'll be fine. They're not connected to me enough for someone to go after them."

The drugs were making her sleepy, and she didn't have the energy to fight against it.

"I really don't like your world, Daniil. I want out."

She caught a flash of pain cross his face before she closed her eyes and drifted off to sleep.

CHAPTER ELEVEN

After her eyes closed and her body relaxed against his bed, he stayed by her side. The last twenty-four hours had been extremely stressful, and he'd not had the chance to sleep much, which didn't look like it would change anytime soon. He wasn't sure how long the pain meds would keep her under, but he guessed if she woke up to find him sound asleep, she'd sneak off on him. And with no Yury or Viktor here to keep an eye out, she would be able to easily escape. No, he had to stay awake and alert.

At least this morning she seemed to be more herself. Yesterday, she'd been in this strange awake-but-not-awake state that freaked him right out. The doc had said it was shock, that she just needed time and rest, but it was scary seeing her staring out vacantly and not tracking anything at all. He'd stripped her and showered her before he allowed the doc in to look at her. The bruising showed that Rodger had caught her ribs when he'd punched her in the stomach, and he knew they'd ache for a while. Her elbow was also badly bruised. The doc was fairly certain it wasn't broken, but it needed to be iced. He'd done as the doctor had ordered and this morning, he was sure there was no break.

Groaning, he forced himself to roll over and leave her to sleep in peace. He made his way down to the ground level of his home and stopped short when he found Yury in the kitchen, drinking a beer. And looking more worn out that Daniil felt, which was saying something.

"What do you have for me?"

While he'd been babysitting Julietta, Yury had been down in the basement taking care of their newest guests. His friend stretched his neck out then took another long pull of his beer before he looked over at Daniil.

"Rodger's a fuckwit. After you cut him off, he went to Tony."

Yeah, because Tony was one of a very few who'd dare to refuse his little announcement about doing business with Rodger. "Predictably, he lost the money, and Tony offered him a deal to pay it back."

"Let me guess? He needed to deliver Julietta to him?"

Yury tilted his beer toward him as he nodded. "You got it. Tony told him once they had her, he'd let Rodger fuck her as much as he wanted, so long as he was rough and let Tony film it. Bastards were planning on sending you some new viewing material."

Anger heated his blood, but he kept it under wraps at this point. "And what did Tony have to add to that little story?"

"Mainly he confirmed what Rodger had said, but also threw in a few other details. Like the fact Rodger told your girl about what you really do for a living. Stupid fucker couldn't wait to tell me how you'd never get near her again after what they told her about what you do. Not sure what kind of damage they've done inside her head, D., especially considering what you pulled before this shit went down. You might be best to cut her loose and move on."

The very thought of losing Julietta had his gut twisting in knots. With a growl, he spun and after snatching up a chair, threw it against the wall, shattering the thing.

"She's mine. I'm not losing her over this shit. No way."

Yury was nodding at him, in that slow way people did when they thought a person was crazy.

"Okay, so you're not cutting her loose. In that case, you better start thinking of ways to suck up to her, because if those two told her all you're capable of, she's going to look at you like you're a monster now."

He winced. He'd thought she'd still been in shock earlier, but maybe it wasn't anything medical. It was simply she was overloaded and not sure what to think about him. How the fuck was he going to fix this shit?

"I'll work something out. You heading over to the hospital now, or are you still working?"

"Yeah, I was going to go check in with Viktor, see if he's awake yet." He paused to drink the last of his beer. "They're still breathing, if you want to go down there and work out some tension. Figure they can wait a few days before we finalise things. Bastards deserve to suffer, and if for some reason Viktor doesn't make it, I want to be able to take my time pulling those fuckers apart."

Daniil shook his head on a dark chuckle. This was why he, Viktor, and Yury had bonded so well. They were made from the same cloth. Before he could respond, his phone rang. He pulled it out and when he saw it was a local number he didn't know, he answered it. He didn't normally, but with Viktor in the hospital and shit going down all over the damn place, he didn't want to risk not taking the call.

"Mikhailov."

"Um, hi. Is this Daniil?"

The female voice was familiar, but he couldn't place it. "Yes, that's me. Who is this?"

"This is Jess, Juli's friend. She didn't come home last night. You know anything about that?"

He huffed out a breath, wondering how to respond. Played correctly, Jess could help him get back into Julietta's good graces. He decided some truth wouldn't hurt. Julietta's injuries meant she'd have to tell people something when they saw the bruising. No way would she be able to surf for who knew how long. He needed to call the company she taught for after he finished speaking with Jess to make sure she didn't lose her job for not turning up.

"She was attacked up the coast while she was taking photos. I arrived in time to stop them from taking her, and she's here at my home, recovering."

The string of curses that blasted back at him through the phone was not ladylike in the least, and he grinned. Girl had some fire in her.

"I thought you had a bodyguard on her all the time! Where the fuck was *he* when this happened?"

"I don't know what happened exactly, but when I arrived, my man had been shot and was unconscious. He's still in the hospital."

That left her groaning. "Can I come see her? Or is your place some super-secret location I'm not allowed to know?"

Apparently, she was a brave little thing as well as having some fire. That was good. He was grateful his Julietta had someone like Jess standing beside her.

"I'm sure she'd love you to visit. Maybe you could bring her a few changes of clothes? I would like her to stay here until she is fully healed."

He gave her his address and hung up before turning to find Yury still there.

"Weren't you going to the hospital?"

Yury shrugged, a little too casually. "I'll wait until Jess gets here. Make sure no one else sneaks in the gates when she comes through. Then I'll go."

He frowned at his friend, but when the man stayed silent, he didn't push things. Time would tell if Yury's reason for hanging around was to protect his boss and friend, or to check out Julietta's friend.

Things could get interesting.

Julietta's body stiffened, and she held her breath when fingers stroked over her cheek and tucked hair behind her ear. Had Daniil returned? What would he want now? Rodger's words played through her mind. Was Daniil really only wanting to put her to work on her back?

"Oh, babe, what the fuck happened this time?"

Her breath whooshed out at the sound of Jess's voice. She blinked open her eyes to find her friend lying beside her on the mattress, head on the pillow in front of hers. Tears pricked Juli's eyes, and when the first one leaked out, Jess shuffled closer and wrapped her arm around to hug her in close. Juli rested her forehead against her friend's as she shuddered with sobs.

"Shhh, you're okay. It's all over, and you're safe now."

She shook her head, and after a few minutes, managed to contain her crying enough to pull back a little and speak.

"No, it's not. Nothing is okay. Not even a little bit."

Jess pulled a tissue from somewhere and wiped Juli's face clean.

"Tell me all that happened, and let's see if we can work out a way to make it right. Sound good?"

Huffing, she looked into her best friend's eyes. Where to start? It was like this latest crap was just the icing on the cake of her shitty life.

"You know, I've often wondered if there was something wrong with me. Like, maybe if I was better, more lovable, Mum wouldn't have killed herself like she did."

Shock rippled over Jess's face. "Oh, sweetheart, I had no idea you were still struggling with your mum's death. It wasn't your fault at all. That was all on her. She's the one who couldn't love. You're totally lovable. Not only are you beautiful and have great tits, but you're funny as hell and always smiling. Everyone you meet loves you."

She scoffed at that. "Yeah, I'm so lovable Rodger only wanted me for my *great tits* and my money. Hell, strangers regularly think I'm nothing more than a nice rack and tight arse."

More tears leaked out, and a sob cut off anything else she was going to say.

Jess pulled her in again for another hug, rubbing her palm up and down her back to soothe her as she cried some more.

"Babe, those strangers are just arseholes.

They don't know a single thing about you, and you shouldn't let their opinions matter to you at all. I guarantee you that your opinion doesn't matter to them. Rodger's nothing but an abusive addict. Gambling isn't so different to drugs. Once addicted, a person changes. The only thing an addict like him truly loves is the thrill of whatever vice they're hooked on. Focus on the people who do care. I've been by your side for nearly twenty years, and nothing is ever going to cut me out of your life, babe. I love you like a sister. In fact, I totally love you more than my sister. She's a bitch, while you're a sweetheart."

That had Juli chuckling a little. Jess was right. Her baby sister was a spoiled brat of the highest order and such a bitch.

"And what about Daniil? He's saved your arse how many times now? Men don't do that for just anybody, especially men like him. You know I hear all sorts of shit in the salon, and from what I've heard, that man doesn't date. Ever. He's a fuck 'em, then leave 'em kinda man. But with you, he's had to work bloody hard to even get you to go to dinner with him. You're so fucking lovable you've converted a silver fox man-whore into boyfriend material. Be proud!"

She knew Jess was trying to make her laugh, but that one was a little too close to the bone.

"Rodger told me what Daniil does for a living, like, the non-legit stuff. He's a criminal, and kills people, maybe even sells them. I don't want to be here with him."

Jess wiggled back a little so she could hold her gaze.

"Okay, firstly, as I've mentioned before, Rodger is an arse wipe. Nothing he says is worth even listening to. Secondly, I've just sat down and had coffee with Daniil. He's really worried, and he cares about you. A lot. He has the money and time to keep you cared for and protected while you heal. In your shoes, I'd stay here and soak it all up while I could. He hasn't hurt you, has he? Tried to rape you?"

Jess's raised eyebrow indicated she already knew the answer.

"No, he's not done anything to hurt me. But I know he's killed men. He's admitted it to me. What happens if I make him mad?"

Jess chuckled. "Babe, trust me. You've

frustrated him plenty in the last week or so, and what has he done? He's sent you flowers and presents. That man is whipped so badly it's not funny. And yeah, he's a criminal. Hell, he's one of the Kings of Sydney, babe. Men don't get to that position by polishing their saintly halos at every turn. But if he was going to hurt you in some way, or use you, he would have done it by now. Hell, he could have snatched you that first day you met at the markets, and no one would have known what happened to you. But he didn't. How about you ask the man directly what his plans for you are, rather than take the word of your ex, who you *know* lies and cheats?"

Juli sighed heavily. "Yeah. I hear you. But right now, it's all too much. I don't want to deal with any of it. I know it's not like me, but I kinda just want to hide from the world and lick my wounds for a while, you know? Worry about all this shit some other day." *When I find the will to keep going, even though I have nothing much left in my life worth living for.*

"You go for it, babe. After all the shit you've been through, I'm surprised you haven't cracked before now. You take all the time you need. I'll be right here for you, ready to help however I can."

After that, they just lay there silently. Jess stroked her hair and face a little, and when she began to rub her back, Juli drifted off to sleep again.

CHAPTER TWELVE

A week later, Daniil was ready to explode. He'd only managed to keep Julietta with him for two days before she'd begged Jess to take her home. He wanted to be the one who comforted her, but he'd been eavesdropping on the conversations the girls had been having each day when Jess came to visit, and he understood his Julietta needed time to heal and recover. This wasn't just about him and the latest attack, it was about her whole world crashing down around her. How recent events had obviously brought up things she'd not dealt with regarding her mother's death, and, of course, being duped by Rodger clearly had her reeling.

From the moment he'd met her, he

admired her inner light and spark. Then as he learned more, he marvelled at her strength to keep staying positive through everything life had thrown at her. But it seemed this latest attack had been too much and she'd shattered. Since she'd gone back to live with Jess, he'd visited each day, but she barely moved. It took both him and Jess to coax her into eating the smallest of meals, and for the most part, she simply stayed curled up in her bed, refusing to talk to or look at anyone. He'd climbed in with her a few times, spooning up behind her so he could hold her close to him. Each time he had, she'd snuggled back into him with a sigh, but that was all the reaction he got. It was breaking his heart to watch her fade away.

Because he'd never before cared for a woman like he did for Julietta, he had no experience in how to handle this situation. Nor did he have anyone in his life he could ask for advice. No parents or grandparents. He tried to think back over his childhood, to the things his father had done for his mother when she'd been unhappy. But he couldn't remember either of his parents ever being anything other than content and happy with life.

What he did know was that previously, she had sought solace in her photography and in the attack, her camera equipment had been smashed beyond repair. So, today he was going to try a different tactic with her. No more coddling. She needed to get out of that tiny room and get some fresh air into her lungs. Remember why life was worth living.

It was mid-morning Sunday when he arrived at her place, and Jess let him in with a grim smile. He winced as he realised she'd missed another week of work and opening her stall at the markets. Of course, he'd contacted both the surf school and the market organisers to explain the situation and pay them enough to hold open her job and site, but that wouldn't make any difference if she couldn't find a way to fight her way back to the land of the living.

"Morning, D."

If he wasn't so worried for Julietta, he'd have laughed at the way Jess was now using the nickname Viktor and Yury used for him most days.

"No change?"

She shook her head, looking sad. "Nope. She's still in her room. I haven't gone in there yet this morning."

He nodded. "I'm taking her out today."

Jess's eyes widened. "Not sure she'll go for that, but good luck."

He grinned. "I don't intend on giving her a choice. Well, she'll get a choice on whether she goes in whatever she's currently wearing, or if she wants a shower and to get changed first. But that's the end of her choices."

Jess' body shook with laughter. "Can I video this? Because her reaction is gonna be priceless."

Pain shot into his heart. "No videos, and as much as the old Julietta would have lashed out at me, this new, depressed version of her probably won't do much at all. I almost wish she *would* lash out."

Jess didn't respond, which didn't surprise him. What could either of them say? Their strong, beautiful girl was fading right before their eyes.

He headed to Julietta's room, knocking lightly before he entered. Another shot of pain pierced his heart. She lay on the bed, but the room was so dark, he could barely make out her form under the blankets. The air in the room was stale and smelled bad enough he rubbed a hand under his nose. *Damn.*

He went to the window and opened the blinds, allowing bright sunlight into the space. He slid the window open, taking a deep breath of the fresh air before he turned to face his girl. She lay facing him but had put a hand over her face, he guessed covering her eyes from the sudden light he'd inflicted on her. Her purple-blue hair that normally looked bright and full of life, lay limp around her head in a mess.

"C'mon, *krasivaya*, time to get up. We're going out."

She separated her fingers and glared at him but stayed silent. He refused to give in, no matter how much he wanted to go curl up behind her and simply hold her close. Folding his arms across his chest, he stared at her.

"Either you get up and go shower and change, or I'll carry you out to the car as you are. Your choice."

She scoffed at him, and he thought he caught a glimmer of humour in her eyes before she rolled onto her front, burying her face in her pillow with a groan. He moved toward her, gently gripping her shoulder to roll her over. He brushed her hair away from her face before he leaned in to press a kiss to her forehead.

"Help me help you. You know a shower will make you feel better, and then I have a surprise that I know you'll love."

"You're not going to give up and go away, are you?"

"Never."

He lowered his mouth to hers, kissing her. He'd barely pressed his lips against hers when she groaned and pulled away, covering her mouth with her hand.

"My breath has to be horrendous."

Her animated reaction had his hope blooming that she was ready to come back to the world of the living. He'd missed her so much this week, and had been aching for the torment she was going through.

He pulled back and ran his knuckles down her cheek.

"It'll take more than some morning

breath to get me to leave you. It's time, my Julietta. You've got twenty minutes to shower and dress, and then we're leaving. And we *will* be going out. Don't think I won't come in here and carry you out in whatever you happen to be wearing when it's time to go."

With that, he gave her another quick kiss before he strode out of her room and back toward the kitchen, hoping Jess wouldn't mind him joining her for a coffee while he waited.

"How'd it go?"

He shrugged. "Find out in twenty minutes. However, I'm optimistic she won't be going out in her pyjamas."

And that was the truth. The way she'd kissed him back was the most life she'd shown since the attack, and it gave him hope things would be okay. Because over the past week, he'd come to realise he'd fallen completely in love with his little surfer. No way did he want to live his life without her in it, so he needed to make certain she got strong again, and then he would set about winning her heart and making her his forever.

Because Juli didn't doubt for a moment Daniil would drag her arse out of the house in her pyjamas, she hauled herself out of bed. Sitting on the edge of her mattress, she ran a fingertip over her lips. They were still tingling from his powerful kisses. A little sigh escaped her. The man could certainly kiss, that was for sure.

Groaning, she stood and grabbed a pair of panties and a maxi-dress with a built-in shelf bra because that was about all her energy level could handle at the moment. Then she headed to the shared bathroom.

Twenty minutes later, she entered the kitchen feeling a lot better than she had all week. She couldn't remember when she'd last showered, and it felt good to be clean from head to toe and in fresh clothes. She wasn't sure what Daniil had planned for their day, but she really didn't want to be around a whole heap of people. Fuck, she hoped he wouldn't be mad with her if she couldn't handle whatever he'd planned and begged to come home.

"Hey, babe!"

Jess tackle-hugged her before she could make it more than two steps inside the room. Juli gave her friend a couple of awkward pats on the back before she tried to pry free.

"How you feeling? Better? Damn, but it's good to see you up and around!"

She shrugged, feeling a little like a science experiment. "Could use a coffee."

Distraction. She needed to get Jess' focus off her. Daniil strode across the kitchen to her, cupping her cheek as he lowered his face and kissed her again. With her palms on his chest, she leaned into him, moaning when he nipped her lower lip before he pulled back. Dropping his arm so he could wrap it around her waist, he brought up his other hand, which held his own coffee.

"Drink mine, *krasivaya*, and then we'll head out."

She took the warm mug from his hand, and a thrill ran through her as she put her mouth where he'd had his and drunk his coffee. It was bitter on her tongue, but she didn't complain. Normally she added milk and sugar to her brew, but this dark, unsweetened coffee was exactly what she needed this morning. She didn't need sweet, not when harshness was her new reality, so the drink was perfect.

Daniil kept his arm around her, holding her close as she drank the rest of his coffee. The gentle strokes he was making over her lower back and upper edge of her arse had all sorts of sensations running through her body. Apparently, her libido had forgiven him and wanted more of what she knew he could give her. Her mind was still on the fence about whether he was forgiven, though.

The moment she drunk the last mouthful, he took the mug, handed it to Jess, then dragged her out the door before she could even say bye to her friend. She was surprised to see he'd switched out his sleek black SUV for a sexy, little blue Mustang convertible with silver racing stripes. Her knowledge of cars was pretty limited, but even she knew what the little horse on the front meant.

"I didn't know you had a Mustang."

A wide grin spread over his face, and his eyes sparkled a little at her words.

"I've had this baby for about a year now,

but I don't get to drive it much. It's not all that practical for a lot of things."

With a palm on her lower back, he guided her around to the passenger side and opened the door before holding her hand as she sat down. She closed her eyes when he leaned in to press a kiss to her forehead. There was something about the way he did it that settled her somewhere deep inside. A minute later he was in the driver's seat, and they were off.

She was grateful she'd taken the time to braid her hair after her shower, as it meant she could enjoy the wind in her face without worrying about her hair flying around. As he drove them further north, up the coast, she relaxed into the seat, closing her eyes and taking deep breaths of the sea air. She must have dozed off because she woke with a start when the car's engine turned off. Jerking in the seat, she sat up straighter and looked around.

"Stay there a minute, I just need to grab something."

She nodded as she continued to stare at the sights around her. It made her miss her camera. Daniil had brought her up to Mystics

Beach in Minnamurra. It was a beautiful white sandy beach that wasn't nearly as busy as Bondi. She couldn't see it from the carpark, but she'd been here before so she knew what was just through the trees. She glanced around, pleased to see only two other cars. She hoped that meant they'd have the beach mostly to themselves.

When he slipped back into the driver's seat, he had a wrapped box. She frowned at it, then him.

"What's that?"

"Just a little something I thought you might like."

Curiosity had her tearing the paper way like an excited toddler. She swallowed past a sudden lump in her throat at the case that was revealed. It was a sleek, metal, high-end camera case. She'd drooled over similar cases online but couldn't justify buying one. Running her palms over the smooth surface, she flicked her gaze up to Daniil's face. He was grinning at her, looking like a cat that had gotten all the cream.

"What did you do?"

He nodded to the case. "Open it up and you'll see."

Excitement had her heart racing. Daniil didn't do presents by halves. Her flowers had always arrived in fancy vases. The necklace he'd sent her was from Hardy Brothers, and when she'd checked their website, had discovered he'd spent around two thousand dollars on the gorgeous yellow gold and diamond creation. She raised her fingers to play with the dozen or so different sized hoops of gold that made up the pendant she was wearing. His gaze tracked her fingers, his expression turning to one of pride and desire.

This man confused her so much. He was extremely ruthless, cutting down anyone in his way with brutal force and finality, yet he spoilt her with pretty things and made sure she was protected. Now that her depression fog was finally lifting, she was left with so many questions.

"Open it already, *solnyshka moto*. I want to see your reaction."

Pushing her questions aside to worry about later, she flipped open the latches and opened the case. When she saw the square shape of the camera along with the word "Nikon" on the top of the front of it, her heart stopped beating, her lungs froze, and her fingers shook as she reached forward to hesitantly touch the piece of extremely expensive equipment.

"Breathe, Julietta."

She gulped in a few breaths and wiped the tears from her eyes. This was an insane gift. There was close to, if not more than, ten thousand dollars' worth of camera and lenses in this case. Without pulling it out, she knew this was the Z9 model. She'd seen a review on YouTube of this camera a few months ago and had instantly wanted one. But it had been so far out of her price range, she'd allowed herself to drool for only a little while before trying to forget it existed.

"It's too much! I can't accept this—"

He cut her off by leaning over and kissing her, taking her lips over and over again, until she relaxed and all but melted against the seat.

"You can and you will accept it. Your last camera was broken in the attack, and if it weren't for me, those men wouldn't have been after you. So, you'll let me replace it for you."

She held his gaze, trying to see if he was being truthful. Did he really blame himself?

"Firstly, it wasn't your fault. Rodger was *my* ex, not yours. He's the bastard who sold me out, and it was on his head that I broke my camera. Secondly, this isn't replacing my old Canon. This is so much more than what I had, I'm not sure I can even call it an upgrade. Hell, what's sitting in my lap is most likely worth more than my car!"

With her face in his palms, he closed his eyes and rested his forehead against hers for a moment.

"I'd upgrade that for you, too, if I thought you'd let me. You are the most precious thing in the world to me. I've made several mistakes these past weeks, and in the end, they cost you greatly. When I first saw you, I thought you were pretty, and then when I spoke to you, I realised you were also smart, quirky and fun. From the first day at the markets, you were like a ray of sunshine in my world of shadows. The more I learned about your history, the more I admired you for remaining so happy. For keeping your inner light bright despite all the times you'd been knocked down. Then, last weekend, you had that light stolen from you. I've watched with my heart bleeding all week as you've hidden away and faded from the world. You need to get out and do what you love, and photography is your passion. So, here we are at Mystics Beach, where there is lots for you to photograph, and now you have the best equipment available to do it. Accept the gift, *krasivaya*, and repay me with a smile and letting me witness your light shining brightly again."

Tears were falling freely, and she did nothing to try to stop them. Yeah, he'd been a total douchebag for taking that video of her, but he'd more than made up for it. Especially since he hadn't given up on her. She'd been a miserable bitch all week, pushing away everyone and everything, yet he'd still visited her every day.

"Have you deleted the video?"

He nodded. "Yes, it's gone. I'm so sorry I even took it in the first place. It was such a dickhead move. Am I forgiven?"

With gentle strokes, he thumbed away her tears.

"Yeah, you're forgiven. But if you do

anything like that ever again, I'll cut your balls off. Understand me?"

He chuckled. "I understand. I won't ever be so stupid again unless I want to be castrated. Got it. I know you had other questions you wanted to ask me after the attack. Ask me so I can answer them, and we can move forward past it all."

She turned her face and kissed his palm before pulling out of his grip.

"Rodger told me that you earn most of your income from drugs, gambling and, um... people."

He tilted his head. "People?"

Her cheeks heated. She hated talking about this stuff. "That you get paid to hurt or kill people. Or, ah, sell them."

He blew out a breath. "I am trusting you with my truths, Julietta. Do you understand?"

She nodded and began to wonder if maybe she shouldn't have asked.

"You already know that I've killed men. I've done so to keep you safe. I did that because I care for you and want you protected. Others, who don't have the ability to do that themselves, pay someone like me to do it for them. Understand? But I have never sold or bought a person. I do have morals and lines I won't cross. That is one of them."

She stared into his eyes, trying to gauge if he was telling the truth. "So you've never had anything to do with prostitutes?"

"Ah, Rodger told you I was going to pimp you out, didn't he?" She gave a jerky nod. "While I have used the services of prostitutes in the past, I have never had any under my control. And I would never seduce a woman into my bed for the purpose of turning her into a prostitute."

More heat rushed to her face, and wincing, she looked away from him. She was so stupid for letting Rodger's words get into her head. Now she felt like a bitch for accusing him like she had.

"I'm sorry I even thought you would do that. I do know you better than that. It's just, well, not much in my life has ever gone right. And you showing up with all the shiny, expensive gifts and all your attention and affection? It seems too good to be true. And you know what they say about that."

He cupped her face again, forcing her

gaze up to his. "You've seen for yourself, my life isn't all sunshine and roses, *krasivaya*. But I believe the many benefits outweigh those moments. Hopefully, you see me as one of the benefits, not a disadvantage. There will be times you'll wish you never met me, I'm sure. But I'm crazy about you, and I don't intend to give up until you're mine."

Before she could respond, he leaned in and kissed her again, melting all her thoughts away with his heat. When he pulled back and released her, she needed to change the subject. He was talking long-term, and she wasn't ready for that kind of talk yet. She gazed down at her new camera again.

"You know, even with this awesome little piece of machinery, I'm still screwed." More tears pricked her eyes. "I've missed two markets with no explanation. That not only costs me my site, but basically blacklists me. It could take years to get my spot back."

She didn't say it out loud, but she feared she'd lost her surfing instructor job too. What was she going to do? With no job, Jess could only afford to carry her arse for so long.

Any joy she'd started to feel vanished in an instant, and she just wanted to go crawl back into bed.

"Hey, whatever you're thinking? Stop it. The market organisers know you'll be back and just needed a couple of weeks off. Trust me, your site is safe. Your surfing job is waiting for you too, if you want it. They just need a couple days' notice to fit you back into the roster. Oh, and I slipped Jess some cash to cover your rent, so don't worry about her kicking you out. Although, that might have been a mistake on my part. I probably should have paid her *to* kick you out. Then you'd have to move in with me."

Tears blurred her vision again despite his attempt at humour, and she shook her head.

"See? You're too good to be true."

Yet he was real, and he was hers. And no matter what she tried to tell herself, it was clear he was also rapidly claiming her heart too.

EPILOGUE

TWO MONTHS LATER

Sighing, she leaned back in her seat. Daniil had brought her to Flamma Oceano for dinner again. They came here every Friday night, and Juli had gotten to meet the owner, Nico, a few times. He was about as stereotypically Italian as a bloke could get. However, he was also a total tease and flirt.

"Settle down, Daniil, you know he didn't mean anything by it."

Her boyfriend sat across from her with a thunderous look on his face.

"Oh, he meant it all right. Sweet-talking little bastard is after my woman."

She barked out a laugh. Nico had just delivered their desserts and served hers with a wink before he leaned in to whisper in her ear how easy it was to tease Daniil now that he was dating her. Naturally, her man proved him right by going all growly caveman, mainly because he didn't believe that was all Nico had said. With another sigh, she put her napkin on the table and moved to sit in the seat beside him. Leaning into him so her breasts pressed up against his arm, she reached up and cupped his face, tilting it toward her. Predictably, his gaze flicked down to the now ample amount of cleavage that was pushed up almost out of her sexy, low-cut blue dress.

"The only thing Nico is after is to rile you up, and you know it. He does it every time we come here if he's working."

Daniil grunted, then his expression cleared into something much hotter. She was grateful they had their usual table hidden out on the balcony when he leaned in and took her mouth. His kisses still melted her, body and soul. He ate at her mouth, nibbling her lower lip before pulling back. He kept a palm holding her cheek as he stared into her eyes. She wasn't sure what he was searching for.

"I love you, *solnyshka moto*."

She grinned broadly. She'd always adored the way he called her his sun. But since her attack and bout of depression, it held more meaning because it was Daniil who had cracked her shell and gotten her to step out of her own shadows so she could begin to shine again.

"And I love you, too, *angel moy*."

By the shocked look on his face, she feared her accent was all wrong but she hoped he could work out that she'd tried to call him her angel.

"You've learned some Russian?"

Heat bloomed over her cheeks and down her neck as she shrugged. "Only a couple of words so far. I wanted to surprise you. Did I say it right?"

"Yeah, *krasivaya*, you said it perfectly."

Suddenly, a dark look passed over his face, and her heart skipped a beat.

"What's wrong? Is it Viktor? Did he have a complication?"

Whenever she feared something had gone wrong in his world, her first thought was for Viktor. He'd been shot and hit over the head hard enough to give him a concussion while guarding her. The last time she saw him, he'd seemed well, but head injuries were strange things and shit could go wrong down the track after having one.

With a scoff, Daniil shook his head. "No, Viktor is fine. Well, he's still got that nurse on his case, but he's healthy."

One of the nurses from the private hospital he'd been in had taken a special interest in Viktor. It was going to be fun watching how that situation played out. Maybe she should agree to move in with Daniil so she could watch the show from a closer perspective. These Russian men were hard-headed, and often didn't see what was in front of their noses. She understood how they felt because she was the same way a lot of the time.

He grabbed her right hand and began stroking his fingers along hers, caressing each digit with his own.

"Julietta, these past months we've been really good together, right?"

"Yeeah." She drew out the word, getting increasingly worried. Her mind took a nosedive, and panic had her breath catching in her lungs. Was he breaking up with her?

Had someone else threatened her and he'd finally decided she wasn't worth the effort? "Just tell me what's happened. Has one of Tony's friends come for revenge? Are you trying to get rid of me now?"

She hadn't asked for details, but she knew both Rodger and Tony were dead. Probably out in the ocean somewhere, or in a shark's belly. She didn't feel guilty about either death. They'd made their beds when they attacked her and Viktor. Clearly, they had no qualms in hurting or killing others... Basically, in her opinion, they lived by a code —a totally fucked up one, but still, it was a code—and that code bit them in the arse when they got too big for their boots.

His eyes popped wide open. "What the hell?" He shook his head. "Clearly, I'm not doing this right." Keeping his grip on her hand, he used his other one to reach into his pants pocket. Pulling it free again, he dropped down to the floor onto one knee.

Holy fucking shit. Is he...

"My precious Julietta, I love you. You're my whole world. Will you make me the happiest man alive, and marry me?"

He was. He was totally proposing, not

breaking up with her. Tears stung her eyes, and she started nodding like a crazy woman.

"Yes."

She couldn't get any more words out. After she'd left Rodger, she'd sworn off all men forever. Remembering how her mother had lived her life, on top of her ex hitting her, had cemented the idea she would be better off single. But then this glorious man had come barrelling into her life. He'd saved her life more than once, and continued to shower her with love and affection. He was never too busy to make time for her, no matter what time of day or night. It also didn't hurt that he was the best lover she'd ever had. Her body heated up and grew wet just thinking about the explosive chemistry they had between the sheets. Her man also liked to buy her pretty things all the time, too, and as much as she didn't need all the gifts, it certainly helped her be sure he wasn't interested in her for her money, like her ex. Nope, Daniil was richer than God apparently, and he liked to spend it on pretty things for her. Who was she to complain?

She frowned in confusion as he slipped a stunning yellow-gold ring, naturally with a freaking huge solitaire diamond on it, onto her right ring finger.

"Shouldn't that go on the other hand?"

He shook his head as he rose from the floor to sit beside her again. "In Russia, it's not tradition to give an engagement ring. It's not until the wedding that rings are exchanged. However, I figured you'd like an engagement ring." He shrugged, looking a little sheepish, not an expression she'd seen him wear before. "And I rather like the idea that you're wearing something that clearly shows others you're spoken for." He paused to clear his throat. "I told you how I lost my parents when I was a teen, so there is a lot I don't know about my heritage, but I remember my mother and father both wearing their wedding rings on their right ring fingers. So, if you don't mind, I'd like for you to wear it on the right. You know... only if you're comfortable with it."

He looked into her eyes with a touch of fear in his gaze, as though he were truly concerned she'd think his request silly or something. And the way he *asked* proved he was really nervous. Her man didn't ask for much. Nope, Daniil Mikhailov made demands, and they were met.

She leaned in and gently kissed him, pulling back before he could deepen the kiss.

"I love that you're wanting to include parts of your heritage in our lives. I'm certain your parents would be extremely proud of you for it. I have no family at all, no heritage to fall back on, so I am more than happy to follow you and learn yours. Maybe one day we could go to Russia, and you can show me where you grew up before you came to Australia."

For a moment, she thought she saw a sheen of tears over his eyes, but he pulled her in and kissed her long and slow before she could be certain. He kept at her until she melted against him in an aroused mess.

"I'm taking you home."

She grinned up at him as he took her hand and led her from the restaurant. Yep, her man was back to his usual self. Making demands and expecting them to be obeyed.

Within minutes, Daniil had them home. And it was their home now. His Julietta had been refusing to discuss moving in with him for over a month, changing the subject every time he brought it up. But now she'd agreed to be his wife? There would be no question as to whether she would be moving in with him or not.

"Yury will come with us in the morning to move your stuff over here."

She shook her head with a chuckle as she got out of the car.

"What? You think I'm not serious? I've made it clear I want you here with me all the time, and now you're wearing my ring. That means you want that too."

He'd moved around the car to stand in front of her as he spoke. She smiled up at him like he was a stubborn toddler who didn't want to go to bed or something.

"You know, at dinner you kept asking me so many questions and acting so worried, I was convinced you were going to break up with me. Now you're all back to growly demands, and I actually feel more relaxed, because you're back to normal. Well, normal for you."

He scoffed. They both knew he could demand all he liked. She would always do as she pleased, and he would let her. She was the only person in the world who held any power over him. His Julietta held his heart and his soul, and there was nothing he would not do for his love.

When she smiled up at him sweetly, he growled low in his throat. He knew how much she loved the sound, and he smirked at her when a shiver ran over her body. As he reached for her, she dodged away from his hands.

"I don't think so! Tonight, we're going to actually make it inside. Yury and Viktor don't need another show."

That had him growling again. They'd gotten carried away a few weeks ago, and he'd stripped her on the way up the path to the front door. Unfortunately, his friends had been walking back to their guest house at the time and had seen more of his future bride than they should have. At least his property was big enough and the land around his home was filled with enough trees to prevent anyone outside of the property's fences from seeing them.

When she slipped off her shoes and ran toward the door, he took off after her with a grin. If she wanted a chase, he'd give her one. And when he caught her, he planned on not letting her go. Ever.

He also suspected she would need to call in sick to work tomorrow. She wasn't going to be able to stand on a surfboard by the time he finished with her tonight.

"You can run, my Julietta, but you can't hide."

Her laughter floated back to him as she pushed through the front door. "Now, why wouldn't I want you to catch me? That's the best part!"

She'd barely put her foot on the bottom stair when he caught her. With an arm around her waist, he pulled her back against his front and lowered his mouth to kiss and nip at her neck. Her citrus scent filled his head and lungs, and with a wide grin he swung her up into his arms and prowled up the stairs toward their room with his prize.

For the first time he could remember, he was looking forward to his future with a full heart, and with Julietta as his beacon of light to show him the way.

"I love you, wife."

She'd started undoing the buttons on his shirt as they'd moved but paused at his words.

"Getting ahead of yourself, *angel moy*, we're not married yet."

With a shake of his head, he lowered her feet to the floor beside their bed.

"Semantics, *solnyshka moto*."

Then he made quick work of stripping her bare. Damn, but she really was such a beautiful creature, and she was all his. Fumbling in his haste, he stripped himself between kisses. Then, picking her up, he tossed her on the bed before following her down. He let her have his full weight for a moment, knowing she liked to feel caged in beneath him. He kissed her again, dancing his tongue with hers as he stroked his palm down her side, leaning up enough to be able to tweak her already tight nipple.

He released her mouth with the intention of moving down to suckle on her other breast when she caught his face in her palms. Her blue eyes were clear and focused as she stared straight into his eyes.

"You're my whole world too, you know

that, right? I love you, Daniil, and I can't wait to really be your wife."

He refused to acknowledge the stinging behind his eyes as he leaned in and kissed his girl deeply again. He really was the luckiest man in the world to have caught such a wonderful, beautiful, quirky woman for his soul mate, lover, wife ... and he hoped, God willing, the mother of his children.

Thank you so much for reading Protecting His Queen. I hope you enjoyed reading Daniil and Juli's story as much as I did writing it. Please consider leaving a review.

There will be more Kings of Sydney stories, and to keep up to date with their progress, along with getting a free ebook, please join my newsletter by heading to my website: www.khloewren.com.

BIOGRAPHY

Khloe Wren lives in rural South Australia with her husband, two daughters and an ever changing list of animals!

She started writing in 2013 and has published over 50 books since then in the romantic suspense genre. She writes both paranormal and contemporary stories, including her best selling series Charon MC.

Khloe enjoys writing outside of the box and she loves her heroes strong, and her heroines even stronger.

facebook.com/khloe.wren.3

instagram.com/khloewren

bookbub.com/authors/khloewren

ACKNOWLEDGMENTS

I wrote this book back in 2017, and it was originally published with a small press publisher under the title "Daniil". Before republishing it, I've extensively revised it and changed somethings up (like what Daniil looks like and how old he is, because I fell in love with my cover image).

Unfortunately, I didn't write these little notes for my books that were with publishers, so I'm not sure who exactly helped me with research and other things while I'll wrote it. But I am sure I had help, so to anyone who did, my thanks!

To my editor, Carolyn, and my proofreader, Jen, thanks for another job well done. I appreciate everything you both do.

xo

Khloe Wren

www.ingramcontent.com/pod-product-compliance
Lightning Source LLC
Chambersburg PA
CBHW071158180726
48291CB00007B/2509